A Book of Princes and Princesses

A BOOK OF
Princes and Princesses

Ruth Manning-Sanders

Illustrated by

Robin Jacques

E. P. Dutton & Co., Inc.   New York

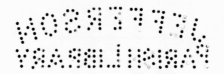

By the same author and artist

A BOOK OF GIANTS

A BOOK OF DWARFS

A BOOK OF DRAGONS

A BOOK OF WITCHES

A BOOK OF WIZARDS

A BOOK OF MERMAIDS

A BOOK OF GHOSTS AND GOBLINS

A BOOK OF PRINCES AND PRINCESSES

J
398.21

First published in the U.S.A. 1970 by E. P. Dutton & Co., Inc.
Copyright © 1969 by Ruth Manning-Sanders
All rights reserved.   Printed in the U.S.A.

FIRST EDITION

Library of Congress Catalog Card Number: 77-102739

Contents

Foreword

Of all the characters found in fairy tales it is the princes and princesses who lead the most adventurous lives. The handsome and valorous prince, before he can win his princess, must go through one perilous adventure after another. He must travel half across the world, lose himself in forests, suffer hunger and thirst, endure utter weariness and near-despair; he must do battle with giants and dragons, outwit wizards, witches, and goblins, prove his manhood in steadfastness, and his courage with his sword. Sometimes he himself falls under a spell, cast upon him by some malignant being; and then it is the princess's turn to rescue *him*, which she does by the magic of her kiss.

As for the princess, though the part she plays is not so active, yet it is not less adventurous. She it is who is snatched away and imprisoned by the dragons, carried off by the ogres and hobgoblins, pursued by the demons, or turned, by the witches and wizards, into some hideous and unnatural shape.

But in the end, of course, it all comes right: the enemy is defeated, the princess freed, and the prince may sheathe his sword; the prince and princess can get married and settle down together to live happily ever after. For in the fairy tale world, however powerful and ugly the evil may be, that evil can never finally stand its ground against the valour of the brave, the good, and the beautiful.

And so you will find, as you read these stories, that they all have one thing in common. Though they come from many different countries, and were told long, long ago by simple people so widely separated that they may not even have known of each other's existence, yet the stories these people told are all alike in this: they every one have a happy ending.

And now to say where the stories come from: *Niassa and the Ogre* comes from Africa; *The Prince and the Sky-Blue Filly* from Yugoslavia; *The Princess's Slippers* from Archangel; *The Wizard King* from Russia; *The Enchanted Prince* from Hungary; *The Frog* from the Ukraine; *The Magic Belt* and *The White Cat and the Green Snake* both from Brittany; *The Prince and the Dragons* from Serbia; *The She-Bear* from Italy; *Princess Felicity* from France; *Rags and Tatters* from Sicily; and the story of *Stupid Head*, which is at least eight hundred years old, from Kashmir.

1 · Niassa and the Ogre

Once upon a time there were two royal children, a little prince called Maran, and a little princess, his sister, called Niassa. And they went out with some other children to play.

Now there was a horrible, horrible ogre who had his eye on princess Niassa; he wanted to catch her and keep her, and make her his wife when she was old enough. So what did he do? He turned himself into a big tree with silver leaves, and set himself down on the grassy plain where the children were playing.

'Oh, see there!' cried Niassa. 'Oh, the lovely tree! Let's climb it and pick some of the pretty silver leaves!'

And she ran to climb the tree, and her little companions did the same.

But her brother, Maran, stood under the tree, and looked up at the branches.

'*What!*' said he. 'Can a tree of that size spring out of the ground in a single hour like a mushroom?'

'Most certainly I can,' said the tree. 'If you wish to pick my leaves you are welcome!'

Then a branch bowed itself down to Maran to invite him to climb up.

'Oh ho!' said Maran. 'A tree that speaks and offers its branches! No, this isn't natural! You others can climb up if you like; but as for me, I stay here.'

So Maran stayed on the ground; and when all the other children were up in its branches, the tree made off, carrying the children with it.

The tree went, went, went, till it came to a cave, and then it

changed back into the ogre. The ogre let the other children go,
but he kept Niassa.

But he was tired, and fell asleep; and when he was snoring
soundly, little Princess Niassa crept out of the cave and ran home.

On another day Maran and Niassa and the other children went
out to play again. What did they see? They saw a big donkey
grazing near them.

'Hurrah!' cried Niassa. 'Let's have a ride!' And she and all the
other children, except Maran, clambered up on to the donkey's
back.

Maran was going to get up too, but there wasn't any more

room on the donkey's back. So what did that donkey do? It made its back longer.

'Oh ho!' said Maran. 'Here is an ass that must be of the same family as the silver-leaved tree! No, I'm not getting up; and you others had better come down.'

But the donkey galloped off, carrying the children with it.

The donkey went, went, went, till it came to the cave; and then it changed back into the ogre. The ogre let the other children go, but he kept Niassa. 'And you don't escape me this time,' said he, 'whether I wake or sleep!' And he put Niassa in a sack, and tied up the mouth of the sack with a thong of bull's hide.

'Now then, sing me to sleep,' said he. And he beat on the sack.

So Niassa sang a sad little song, and the ogre fell asleep.

In the morning he opened the sack and gave Niassa some food. Then he tied up the sack again. 'Since you can sing so prettily, you shall earn a living for me,' said he. And he made himself into the likeness of a pedlar, slung the sack over his shoulder, and off with him to a village. 'I have a bird in my sack,' says he to the villagers. 'Give me some breakfast, and you shall hear my bird sing.'

So the villagers gave him food, and when he had eaten it he beat on the sack and said, 'Sing, sing, my bird!'

And Niassa sang a sad little song.

'Sing a merry song,' said the ogre, and he beat the sack harder.

So Niassa sang a merry song, and she was crying, and the villagers laughed. 'Your bird is a wonderful bird,' said they. 'It can be sad and merry at the same time!'

The ogre went from village to village with his sack. Sometimes he asked for food, sometimes for pennies. He got his pockets full of money. But he would never open the sack for the people to see what kind of a bird he had.

One day he came to the place where the king lived. He put the sack down outside the king's house and said, 'Give me gold and my bird shall sing for you.' The king gave him a piece of gold. The ogre beat on the sack and said, 'Sing, sing, my bird!'

And Niassa sang. And little prince Maran heard and thought, 'Surely that is my sister's voice I hear?' So he said to the king, his father, 'Give the old pedlar plenty to eat and drink, and let him rest here in the courtyard for the night. Because his sack is heavy, and he has walked a long way.'

So they brought the pedlar food and drink, and Maran put a sleeping powder in the drink, and the pedlar fell asleep in the courtyard with the sack beside him. He lay and he snored. No, nothing would wake him.

In the night Maran came and undid the thong from the mouth of the sack, and let out Niassa. 'Run quickly into the house,' whispered he. And Niassa ran quickly, none more quickly. Then Maran fetched his big dog, Bomba, and put him in the sack, and whispered, 'Lie very still, my good dog, Bomba.'

So good dog Bomba curled up inside the sack and lay very still, and Maran tied up the sack with the thong again.

In the morning, there was the pedlar still asleep, and Maran gave him a shaking and said, 'Wake up, old man, we've brought you your breakfast!' So the ogre yawned and sat up and ate; and after that he slung the sack over his shoulder and walked off.

He went to another village, set down the sack, and said to the people, 'I have a bird in my sack. Give me some pennies and my bird shall sing for you.' The villagers gave him some pennies. He beat on the sack. 'Sing, sing, my bird!'

And inside the sack Bomba growled.

'What!' says the ogre. 'Do you dare to disobey me, my bird? Sing, sing, I say!' And he beat the sack again.

And inside the sack, Bomba growled.

'Sing, sing, you rascally bird!' says the ogre, beating on the sack harder and harder. But the harder he beat, the louder Bomba growled.

'Cheat, cheat!' cried the villagers. 'You take our pennies and you give us no song!' And they picked up stones, and stoned the ogre out of the village.

The ogre went back to his cave. He was raging. 'Very well, my bird,' said he, 'now I shall kill and eat you!' And he opened the sack.

'R'r'-ow! R'r'-ow!' Out leaps big dog Bomba. 'R'r'-ow!' Big dog Bomba fixes his teeth in the ogre's leg. The ogre yells, the ogre runs, but big dog Bomba is running too, and he doesn't let go of the ogre's leg until he has bitten a piece clean out of it. The ogre is yelling, big dog Bomba is growling and snarling, he has torn the coat off the ogre's back now, and still they are running, and still the ogre is yelling, and still big dog Bomba is growling and snarling and tearing, and spitting the ogre's clothes out all along the way, till that ogre has nothing on but half a shirt. So then big dog Bomba looses his hold and turns and trots home.

The ogre ran and ran, he was too frightened to stop. But where he went to I can't tell you, because he never came back.

2 · The Prince and the Sky-Blue Filly

There was once a king whose good queen died, and left him with a little son, called Erbyu. And the king spoiled his little son, and let him have his own way in everything.

So the prince's chamberlain came to the king and said, 'Sire, our little prince is getting out of hand.'

The king was in a bad temper that morning. He said, 'Are you telling me that I spoil my son?'

'That is what the nurses are saying, my liege,' answered the chamberlain.

'Then see to him yourself!' snapped the king. And he ordered out his horse. He was going for a long solitary ride to cool his temper.

Now when the king went riding it was his custom to take little prince Erbyn up before him. So when little prince Erbyn saw the horse led out and the king with one foot in the stirrup, he came running into the courtyard laughing and calling out, 'Lift me up, papa, lift me up!'

But the king, being in a temper, gave his foot a jerk. Little prince Erbyn fell down. The king said, 'Be off with you!' and little prince Erbyn went back into the palace and cried bitterly. He couldn't understand it at all.

And the king rode on his way. His temper soon cooled down, but he wasn't happy. 'Heaven help me!' he thought. 'What a wretched fool I am! First I spoil that child, and then I kick him! Who would

14

believe it? If only his dear mother were alive it wouldn't have happened.'

The king almost shed tears then, thinking of his dead queen, and of what a mess of things he was making without her. And by and by he gave a great sigh and said to himself, 'I expect I'd better marry again, and give that child a mother to look after him.'

Now as the king rode on his way, he thirsted, and he came to a well. There was a woman at the well; she had twelve gourds laid out on the grass, and she was filling the gourds with water. And on the grass beside the gourds sat a beautiful little girl of about the same age as prince Erbyn.

The king said, 'I thirst. Give me to drink.'

The woman emptied the water out of one of the gourds, filled it afresh, and offered it to the king. The king drank. Then he said, 'Tell me, good woman, who are you, and why are you filling these twelve gourds with water?'

'Sire, I am a poor widow woman. I fill these gourds with water that I may live. There is no other water so pure and sweet as the water in this well; and for every full gourd that I carry to our village, I receive a penny or a crust of bread. So we live from day to day, my little girl and I.'

Now the woman was bold and handsome, and the king felt compassion for her lot. He thought, 'If I am to marry again, it is all one to me whom I marry. Why not take this woman? She will be a mother to my son, and the little girl will be a playmate for him.'

So he said, 'How would you like to be queen?'

'I should like it well enough,' said the woman.

Done and done! The king rode home, sent a carriage to bring the woman and her child to court, and married her next day. The people were astonished. Nobody liked the new queen; she was vain and selfish, gave herself airs, and treated the courtiers as the dirt under her feet. 'The king must be crazy to choose such a wife!' whispered the court ladies to the court gentlemen.

But there, a queen is a queen, and whatever the lords and ladies thought, they must do her bidding, or she would run with complaints to the king, and get them punished.

The king soon found he had met his match, and more than his match. But the new queen looked after little prince Erbyn, and saw to it that the child was not spoiled. And that was what the king had married her for, wasn't it?

As for the new queen's little daughter, whose name was Gabriella, she was a beautiful and loving child. The king couldn't see enough of her; he would have spoiled her as he had spoiled the little prince, but Gabriella had no use for the king and his foolish ways. It was little prince Erbyn she loved, and little prince Erbyn she wanted to be with. The two children were always together. They shared their toys, they shared their games, they shared their love: they wanted no one but each other.

Did that suit the new queen? No, it did not. She became jealous of Erbyn, she got to hate him, thinking that he came between little Gabriella and herself. And she made mischief with the king, dinning his ears with false tales of Erbyn's bad behaviour, until the foolish king came to dislike his son almost as much as the queen did.

Said the king to himself, 'That boy has always been a nuisance! And now here he is, making trouble between the queen and me! Erbyn, Erbyn – bother Erbyn! Drat the boy! I only want to live in peace!'

So it went on; and Erbyn grew into a fine handsome lad, and Gabriella into a beautiful maiden. They still loved each other better than anything else in the world; and it was not in the queen's power to come between them.

Thinks she, 'I must get rid of that lad! And I *will* get rid of that lad!'

So that night, when the king was in bed, sound asleep and peacefully snoring, he woke to find the queen shaking him. She was sobbing and lamenting like one gone crazy.

'Hey! What's the matter, what's the matter?' grunted the king.

'Oh, that Erbyn!' cried the queen. 'He will be the death of us all! I have long suspected it, and now I know it!'

'Bother Erbyn! What's he done this time?'

'My dream!' wailed the queen. 'My awful, awful dream! I dreamed that Erbyn rushed at your throne with a hatchet and chopped it into little pieces. And then he struck you on the head with the hatchet and killed you! I saw you lying dead at my feet! He seized your kingdom for himself, and drove me and my Gabriella to work in the kitchen!'

This was too much for even the foolish king to swallow. Besides, he was vexed at being so roughly wakened. So he said, 'Silly woman! Don't you know that dreams go by contraries?'

'Oh, so dreams go by contraries, do they?' said the queen. 'And that's all the thanks I get for warning you! But warn you I must and shall, for it is my duty. And one day you'll be sorry you didn't believe me!'

'Now do leave me in peace!' said the king.

But she didn't leave him in peace. Night after night she pretended to dream of Erbyn's crimes; and night after night she woke the king to tell him these dreams. Till one day the king flew into a passion and went to Erbyn and shouted, 'Get out of my sight before you drive me mad!'

'But, my father, what have I done?'

'Done! Done! How should I know what you've done? I only know that I can't bear the sight of you!'

'Then I will try to keep out of your way, my father.'

But no, that wouldn't do. Erbyn might keep out of the king's way, but as long as he remained in the palace he couldn't keep his name out of the queen's mouth; and so the king told him, using rough and unkind words.

'Then I have my stepmother to thank for this?' said Erbyn.

'I don't care whom you have to thank!' shouted the king. 'Get out, before I am tempted to run my sword through your body!'

17

Prince Erbyn went sadly away. He walked out of the palace, out of the city, on and on, without looking back. He took nothing with him, not even money in his pocket. He was sore, sore at heart; and what troubled him more than all was that he hadn't been able to bid Gabriella goodbye, because the queen had kept her shut away out of sight.

Now no sooner had the king come out of his temper, than he was sorry for what he had done. And he sent a messenger galloping after Erbyn to bid him come back. But Erbyn was proud.

Said he, 'I am setting out on heroic adventure. I will not come back until I have proved my mettle. Tell this to the king, my father. Only I pray you carry to the princess Gabriella my undying love.'

So the messenger galloped back to the palace, and Erbyn walked on. He walked right out of his father's kingdom; and he was hungry and footsore. So, in a desert place, he came to a little hut, and knocked.

An old hermit opened the door.

Said the hermit, 'What would you, my son?'

Said Erbyn, 'Somewhere to lay my weary bones for the night, little father. And a morsel to eat, if you can spare it.'

The hermit took the prince in, shared with him his supper of bread and milk, and shook down a bundle of straw for him to sleep on.

In the morning, when Erbyn was ready to go, he thanked the hermit and said, 'Will you bless me, little father?'

And the hermit answered, 'Right willingly do I bless you, my son. And I would bestow on you a gift, did I know what you most desire.'

'Some comfort for a sorrowing heart is all I desire, little father.'

The hermit opened a box, took out a flute, handed it to the prince, and said, 'Here is your comfort, my son.'

The prince didn't see what comfort a flute could bring him. But he put the flute in his pocket, thanked the hermit, and went on his way. He crossed the desert and came to a little wood; and there, under the shade of a tree, he sat him down.

He was sorry, sorry for himself, alone in the wide world, without money, without a friend, and far, far from his beloved Gabriella. He took the flute out of his pocket and said, 'Little flute, since you cannot comfort me, you shall at least give voice to my sorrow.'

And he put the flute to his lips to play a melancholy tune.

But what's this? What's this? The flute refuses to play a melancholy tune. It's playing a tune so merry, so comical, so full of life and joy, that it would make a body laugh to hear it. And the prince *did* laugh. He forgot his sorrow, he jumped to his feet and began to dance: yes, there on the edge of that desert, driven out, friendless, alone, without a penny in his pocket, he was actually laughing and dancing merrily to the merry piping of the flute.

'*Tee hee! Tee hee!*' Up on a branch of the tree a squirrel is laughing and dancing too.

'*Chiree, chiree, chee! Chiree, chiree, chee!*' A flock of little birds fly down, fluttering their wings and dancing round the prince.

'*Ha! ha! ha! Ho! ho! ho!*' It seemed to the prince that the whole world was dancing, and the trees in the wood were laughing fit to burst.

When he stopped playing, and put the flute in his pocket again, all was quiet. But his sorrow had gone from him, and he went on his way with a merry heart.

In the afternoon he came to a large manor house, surrounded by barns; and from the barns came the bleating of many sheep. The prince thought, 'This is the first time I have known of sheep penned up indoors whilst the sun is yet shining! Do they lack a shepherd here, I wonder?'

So he goes on past the barns and comes to the house itself. And there is the lord of the manor standing on the doorstep. The prince takes off his cap and bows low. 'My lord,' says he, 'are you in need of a shepherd to drive your flocks to pasture? If so, I am in need of a job, and would gladly serve you.'

'My good lad,' says the lord of the manor, 'you don't know what you ask! Alas, alas, no man on earth can drive my sheep to pasture and bring them safely home again. And so I must keep them shut up by day and by night, and feed the poor beasts on cut grass as best I may.'

The prince said, 'That doesn't sound right or natural.'

'It is not right, nor is it natural,' said the lord of the manor. 'But what can I do? In yonder mountain lives a giant, and if my poor sheep but put their noses out of doors, down comes the giant and carries them off.'

The prince said, 'Give me a good sword and I will kill that giant!'

And the lord of the manor answered, 'Other men have tried to kill him, but all have failed. For he has a body so iron-hard that no sword can pierce it. He would but pick you up together with the sheep, carry you off to the mountain and make a meal of you.'

'Nevertheless, I pray you let me drive your sheep to pasture,' said the prince. 'For I know a trick would foil that giant.'

The lord said no and no and no. He said it many times. But the prince was not to be denied, and he got his way in the end. But first he got a good meal and a good bed, and rose in the morning, gay as a lark.

So, after a good breakfast, he set off driving part of the flock, for the lord wouldn't let him take them all.

'Oh, my poor sheep, my poor sheep!' said the lord. 'Don't drive them far! Keep to the nearer pastures, so that whilst the giant is snatching some, you may perhaps at least escape home with a remnant.'

But what does the prince do? He drives the flock to the very foot of the giant's mountain, where the grass is greenest and sweetest. And the sheep have scarcely begun to nibble that grass, when the earth shakes and the mountain trembles, and down strides a giant so huge that his head seems to touch the sky.

And the giant flings out his great hand and begins scooping up the sheep, twenty at a time.

'Hey!' cries the prince. 'Hands off my sheep!'

The giant stooped, peered at the prince out of eyes as big as mill wheels, and let out a laugh that set the mountain echoing.

'What, manikin, what?'

'Hands off my sheep!'

The giant laughs some more, and goes on scooping up the sheep, and stuffing them into an enormous sack slung at his waist. 'You'd best be getting home, manikin,' roars he, 'or you'll find there's room for you in my sack along with your sheep!'

But the prince took the flute from his pocket and began to play. What happened? The sheep – those that were not in the sack – began to dance, and the giant began to dance, and the prince began to dance: but he went on playing.

At first the giant thought it great fun; he laughed till the world echoed. But by and by he grew tired and bawled out, 'Enough! Enough!'

'Give me back my sheep then,' cries the prince.

'Not I!' bawls the giant.

So the prince goes on playing, and the giant goes on dancing. Until, by and by, 'Stop! Stop!' he shouts. 'If you will but stop I'll give you my best horse!'

'Put down my sheep!'

'I'll give you a magic sword and a suit of silver armour!'

'Put down my sheep!'

And all this time the prince went on playing; and the giant danced, and the sheep danced, and the prince danced. And the giant, being so huge and heavy, tired before the prince. He fell flat on the ground, but still his legs went on dancing; he leaped up again, and still he was dancing. And at last he bawled out, 'Stop! Stop! I shall die! I shall die!'

'I'll stop if you put down my sheep.'

'You miserable little manikin!' panted the giant. 'Here – take your sheep!'

So the prince stopped playing, and the giant began lifting the sheep out of the sack, and setting them down one by one on the grass. But he tried to keep some sheep back.

'All of them,' says the prince. 'Or you dance again.'

'No! No!' howls the giant. And he toppled the rest of the sheep out of the sack, and turned the sack inside out to show the prince that it was empty.

'Now,' says the prince, 'where's that horse you promised me?'

'You've got your sheep,' says the giant. 'You can't have the horse as well.'

'Oh, can't I?' says the prince.

And he puts the flute to his lips.

So then the giant rushed up the mountain, and came rushing down again, leading a sky-blue filly with a silver star on her forehead.

'And the suit of armour and the magic sword?' says the prince.

'I'll own you've beaten me,' says the giant. And off he rushes up the mountain again, and comes back with a rusty old sword and some battered armour.

'Cheat!' cries the prince. 'These aren't what you promised me!'

So he begins to play the flute again. The sky-blue filly dances, the sheep dance; the giant sheds tears and goes dancing away up the mountain, and comes dancing down again with a sword in a silver scabbard, and a suit of shining armour.

'Now,' says the prince, 'off with you to the other side of the world! And when you come back, you shall have another tune.'

The giant runs off; he never stops running till he gets to the other side of the world. And from the other side of the world he hasn't come back yet. As for sheep, he hasn't dared to look one in the face again; and the sight of a shepherd makes his huge body tremble like a jelly.

And under the mountain, in the green meadows, the sheep wandered at will until sunset. Then the prince put on the suit of silver armour, buckled the magic sword at his belt, jumped on to the back of the sky-blue filly, and drove his flock back to the manor.

The lord of the manor had spent a miserable day. When he saw the prince coming with the sheep, he jumped for joy. 'I can't believe it! I can't believe it!' he cried.

'The giant has gone to the other side of the world, and he's not coming back,' said the prince. 'The merest child can now shepherd your flocks in safety. But as for me, I have won my armour and my sword and my sky-blue filly; and tomorrow I set out in search of heroic aventures.'

'I see you are no common lad,' said the lord of the manor.

'Nay, I am a prince, though an unfortunate one.'

'Then I may not urge you to stay with me,' said the lord. 'For all I could offer you is not worthy of a prince.'

You may be sure that the prince was honoured and feasted that night, and given the best room in the manor to sleep in. And in the morning early, he said goodbye to the lord of the manor, and rode on his way.

It would take too long to tell of all the prince's heroic adventures. He fought with demons, he rescued distressed maidens from witches and ogres, he slew hundreds of dragons, he defeated rebel armies and set rightful kings on their thrones again. All the world must dance to his piping, should he so choose it; and what his flute could not accomplish, his magic sword achieved. The world rang with his praises. Many a kingdom was offered to him, many a lovely princess was his for the taking. But he refused all and went on his way, forever true to his dear love, Gabriella.

So one day, as he was riding along a lonely road, the sky-blue filly said, 'Master, where are we going?'

'Nay, I know not,' said the prince.

'It would be well to return to your father's kingdom,' said the sky-blue filly.

'Not I!' said the prince. 'There I will never go, until my father bids me welcome.'

'Your father's kingdom is in sore distress,' said the sky-blue filly. 'A dragon has come out of the sea to ravage the country. Many a man has sought to kill this dangerous dragon; none has succeeded. He has taken his toll of beasts and men; now he would take his toll of maidens. The princess Gabriella has offered herself as a ransom – '

But the prince didn't wait to hear another word; he turned the head of the sky-blue filly, and there he is, off galloping faster than fast in the direction of his father's kingdom.

Up hill, down dale, over seven times seven mountains, through seven times seven forests he galloped: the earth fled away behind him, cities sprang up and vanished, rivers glittered and faded, crowds gathered and melted; not once did he pause in his galloping till he came to the shores of his father's kingdom; and there on the edge of the sea he drew rein and looked about him.

'That was a hard run, my master,' said the sky-blue filly.

The prince looks over the sea. There, with his flat cruel head resting on the little waves, is the dragon, sleeping off his latest meal of the king's subjects.

The prince cups his hands to his mouth and shouts, 'Dragon! Dragon! Come out and fight!'

The dragon heard, the dragon came; he came breathing out flames, and lashing the sea with his spiked tail. He came right out of the water, and rushed at the prince with a terrible roar.

The prince drew his magic sword and thrust it into the dragon's mouth. The dragon snapped his teeth, the sword blade shivered, the dragon chewed it up. And the prince is left with only the broken hilt.

'Ha! ha! ha! little princeling,' roars the dragon. 'Come between my teeth and join your sword!'

But the prince put his flute to his lips. He began to play, and the dragon began to dance. He was dancing round the sky-blue filly now, and the sky-blue filly was dancing also; the waves were dancing, the clouds were dancing, the whole world was dancing. The dragon's teeth were dancing in his jaws to the time of the flute's playing. He danced and panted and snapped and whirled, and the sky-blue filly danced just beyond his reach.

'Villain!' roared the dragon. 'Stop your piping! I am quailing! I am quailing!'

Yes, the dragon *was* quailing. There, before the prince's eyes, he was growing smaller and smaller. First he was the size of a battleship, then the size of a whale, then the size of a shark, then no bigger than a man, then no bigger than a dwarf. And as he whirls round, so he becomes round: he is a globe, he is a ball, he is a bubble. The bubble dances, the sky-blue filly dances; and the sky-blue filly strikes the bubble with her hoof – and bursts it.

Then the prince puts the flute in his pocket and rides off to his father's palace.

A great crowd went with him, shouting and cheering; for the people had gathered at the top of the beach to watch the battle. 'Hail to the hero! Hail to the mighty hero who has delivered us from the jaws of the dragon!'

The king hears and runs out of the palace. He bows low. He kneels, takes off his crown and holds it up to the prince.

'Take my crown, take my kingdom; but tell me who you are that I may honour you!'

The prince leaped from the back of the sky-blue filly, raised the king, and himself knelt. 'My father, I am prince Erbyn – have you so utterly forgotten me?'

'My son, oh, my son, whom I drove from me! I am ashamed to look you in the face!'

And the king wept.

But the prince Erbyn comforted his father, and they went into the palace together. There was Gabriella, the lovely maiden, coming to greet him.

'My prince!'

'My princess!'

'My true love!'

'My bride!'

They are in each other's arms, and the king is shedding tears of joy.

But the queen had hidden herself. She was howling with rage and disappointment. Better the dragon had eaten them all than that prince Erbyn should have come back in triumph! No, she couldn't bear it! She wouldn't stay to look upon him!

So what did that queen do, but go back to the well. And there, should you seek for her, you will find her to this day, filling her twelve gourds with water, and selling the water for crusts of bread.

And the happy, happy wedding of prince Erbyn and the lovely Gabriella took place amid great rejoicings. Erbyn was crowned king, for his father gave up his throne to him. They were all happy. King Erbyn reigned long and wisely; the lovely Gabriella had a little son and a little daughter as lovely as herself; and the sky-blue filly was given honey-cakes to eat, and a flowery meadow to gambol in.

3 · The Princess's Slippers

Once upon a time a young princess went out to walk in the meadows. And what should she see, curled up on a dock leaf, but a big, big green and gold caterpillar.

'Oh, what a pretty thing you are!' cried the princess. 'I think you will turn into something very beautiful!' And she broke off the dock leaf with the caterpillar curled up on it, and carried it home.

She put the caterpillar in a glass jar, and it lay there munching away at its dock leaf, and getting bigger every minute, till there was no dock leaf left for it to munch. So the princess ran out to pick it some more dock leaves. And it munched and munched and grew and grew until it was as big as the jar. So then the princess put it in a big bowl, and brought it more dock leaves and still more. And it munched and munched and grew and grew until it was bigger than the bowl; and the princess put it in a copper cauldron, and brought it more dock leaves, and still more. And it munched and munched and grew and grew until it had outgrown the cauldron.

So the princess put it in a big chest, and spent all her days running out to gather dock leaves for it. And still it munched, and still it grew, till the chest was too small to hold it. So the princess made a nest of hay for it out in the stable. And still it munched, and still it grew till it was as big as a sheep. And 'Oh! oh!' said the princess, 'when *you* turn into a butterfly, you will be the world's wonder!'

But the caterpillar didn't turn into a butterfly; it just ate itself to death. And the princess ran crying to the king and queen.

'My lovely, lovely caterpillar – it's dead!' she sobbed.

'And a good thing too,' said the queen. 'The creature wasn't natural.'

But the king said, 'Don't cry, little daughter! We'll have the creature skinned, and we'll have the skin dressed, and from the skin the court shoemaker shall make you a lovely pair of slippers.'

'I'd like that,' said the princess. And she stopped crying.

So the caterpillar was skinned, and the skin was dressed, and the court shoemaker made the slippers. They were the most beautiful slippers, all green and gold. The princess puts them on, dances about in them, proud as proud.

The queen said, 'Take off those slippers! They'll bring you bad luck!'

No, the princess won't take them off. She goes on dancing about and singing:

'Oh, my lovely little slippers,
Who in all the world would guess
What you're made of, little slippers?'

'Ha!' says the king. 'That gives me an idea. It's time our little daughter was married.' And he sent out the town criers with their bells:

'Ding-a-ding, ding! Ding, dong! The princess Nastafia has a wonderful pair of slippers, all green and gold. Whosoever can guess what skin those slippers are made of shall have the princess to wife.'

'For the man who guesses *that* riddle will be a clever fellow!' said the king. 'And I should like a clever fellow for a son-in-law.'

'Whoever may be clever, I think *you* are very foolish,' said the queen.

But the princess said, 'Oh, what fun! Only I hope he'll be handsome as well as clever!'

Well, as you may believe, there was no lack of smart young fellows, both rich and poor, coming to the palace to look at the princess's slippers. The princess sat in a silver chair, with her feet on a red velvet cushion, and the smart young fellows trooped in, one after the other, to look at the green and gold slippers and guess what skin they were made of. Some guess this, some guess that; but none of them guess right. And if those smart young fellows came in with high hopes, they go out in bitter disappointment.

'It seems I shan't be married at all!' pouts the princess.

'Of course you'll be married!' says the king. 'These young fellows are all fools. But a clever fellow will come along one day.'

And one day the clever fellow did come along. But, oh dear me, he was a demon. The demon knew at once that the slippers were made of a caterpillar's skin; well, he had put the caterpillar on the dock leaf himself, so he should know. He told the king so, and claimed his bride.

The king wept and tore his beard. The queen wept and scolded. The princess wept and shut herself up in her room. But a king must keep his word: the wedding day is fixed; and that day comes nearer and nearer.

Now the queen had a pet billy goat. And very early on the wedding morning, even before the sun had risen, she went to the billy goat and said, 'Do you love our little princess?'

And the billy goat answered, 'Yes, I love her.'

So the queen fetches the princess, who had spent the night crying, puts her on the billy goat's back, covers her up with a bundle of hay, so that not even her head is showing, and says, 'Billy goat, billy goat, take her away!'

And the billy goat scampers off.

The long table was set up in the hall for the wedding feast; the queen bade the servants bring in a scarecrow, with a turnip for a head. She dresses the scarecrow in the princess's bridal robes, puts it to sit at the top of the table, and covers its turnip head with a bridal veil. In this manner she hoped to deceive the demon, at least for a little while, until the princess had got safely away.

Meanwhile the demon had set out in style to ride to the palace, dressed like a lord in scarlet and gold, and with three carriages full of lesser demons, also splendidly dressed, going in procession before him.

And as this procession is coming along the king's high road, it meets the billy goat with his load of hay.

The first carriage pulls up. A demon puts his head out of the window and says:

> *'Billy goat, billy goat,*
> *With your heavy load of hay,*
> *You shake your little head,*
> *You wag your little beard,*
> *Tell us, and tell us truly,*
> *Is the princess at home?'*

31

And the billy goat answers:

> *'At home, at home, at home!*
> *In three ovens she bakes,*
> *Three veils she stitches,*
> *Long since she has awaited you guests.'*

So the first carriage drives by, and the second carriage pulls up. A demon puts his head out of the carriage window and says:

> *'Billy goat, billy goat,*
> *With your heavy load of hay,*
> *You shake your little head,*
> *You wag your little beard,*
> *Tell us, and tell us truly,*
> *Is the princess at home?'*

And the billy goat answers:

> *'At home, at home, at home!*
> *Three cakes she has baked,*
> *Three bridal veils she has stitched,*
> *Long, long she has awaited you guests.'*

The second carriage drives by, and the third carriage pulls up. A demon puts his head out of the window, and says:

> *'Billy goat, billy goat,*
> *With your heavy load of hay,*
> *You shake your little head,*
> *You wag your little beard,*
> *Tell us, and tell us truly,*
> *Is the princess at home?'*

And the billy goat answers:

> *'At home, at home, at home!*
> *Three cakes she has put on the table,*
> *With three bridal veils she has covered her head,*
> *With three white robes she has robed her body,*
> *She awaits, she awaits, she awaits you guests.'*

The third carriage drives by; a diamond coach comes up; the demon bridegroom puts his head out of the coach window:

> '*Billy goat, little billy goat,*
> *With your heavy load of hay,*
> *You shake your little head,*
> *You wag your little beard,*
> *Tell me, and tell me truly,*
> *Is the princess at home?*'

And the billy goat answers:

> '*At home, at home, at home!*
> *Three cakes she has put on the table,*
> *With three bridal veils she has covered her head,*
> *With three white robes she has robed her body,*
> *With three pearl chains she has girdled her waist,*
> *She awaits, she awaits, she awaits her groom.*'

So the diamond coach drove on; and the billy goat, with his heavy load of hay in which the princess was hidden, scampered off in the opposite direction.

The demon came to the king's palace. He jumped out of his diamond coach and said, 'Why isn't my bride at the door to greet me?'

And the queen answered, 'She awaits you in the hall where the feast is spread.'

The demon went into the hall. He saw the scarecrow in its bridal robes seated at the head of the table.

'Rise up, my bride,' said he, 'rise up and salute me!'

No answer.

The demon strode nearer. 'Are you deaf, my bride? Rise up and kiss me!'

No answer.

The demon came up close to the scarecrow and shouted, 'Rise up, my bride, rise up and kiss me!'

No answer.

Then the demon flew into a rage. 'Is this the way you greet your bridegroom, you saucy thing?' And he gave the scarecrow a blow that toppled it over.

Off falls the bridal veil. Down rolls the turnip head. There it lies on the floor, grinning horribly at the demon.

'Ah! Ah!' yelled the demon. 'That billy goat has deceived me! It was *he* who carried the princess hidden under his load of hay!' And he rushed out of the hall, leaped into his diamond coach, and made off at a gallop after the billy goat.

The billy goat was scampering, scampering. The princess spoke out of the bundle of hay:

> *'Little billy goat, little billy goat,*
> *Do I hear the sound of wheels?*
> *Stoop your ear to the ground and listen,*
> *Isn't the demon behind us?'*

The billy goat stooped his ear to the ground and said, 'He comes, he comes, he comes. He is very near!'

'Billy goat, billy goat, what shall I do?'

'Throw down your comb, throw down your comb!'

The princess took a comb from her hair, threw it behind her and said:

> *'May this comb become a wood,*
> *A deep dark pathless wood.*
> *No bird to fly through it,*
> *No beast to run through it,*
> *The demon not to travel through it.*
> *Only in front of* me
> *Let there be*
> *A broad, level way.'*

And there behind her rose a wood: deep, dark, thick-set, with no road through it.

The demon in his diamond coach came up to the wood. He shouted at the coachman to force a way through it. No, it couldn't be done! The horses reared and plunged, neighed and backed. The demon leaped from the coach, drew his sword, hacked, hacked, hacked. He hacked a level way through that wood at last, and the diamond coach drove on.

The billy goat was scampering, scampering. The princess spoke out of the bundle of hay:

> *'Little billy goat, little billy goat,*
> *Do I hear the sound of wheels?*
> *Stoop your ear to the ground and listen –*
> *Is the demon behind us?'*

The billy goat stooped his ear to the ground and said, 'He comes, he comes, he comes. He is already near!'

'Billy goat, billy goat, what shall I do?'

'Throw down a shoe, throw down a shoe!'

So the princess took off one of her shoes and threw it behind her, saying:

> *'May this shoe become a mountain,*
> *And the mountain reach the sky:*
> *No bird to fly over it,*
> *No beast to climb over it,*
> *The demon not to get over it.'*

And there behind her rose a mountain, high, high, with its head hidden in the clouds, and sides so steep and slippery there was no climbing them.

The demon in his diamond coach came to the mountain. He shouted at the coachman to drive up it. The coachman set his horses at the mountain; he set them at it again and again. But their hoofs can't grip its slippery sides: they slide back, they rear, they plunge, they snort. No whippings, no shoutings, nothing avails. So the demon leaps out of the coach, draws his sword, hacks,

hacks, hacks at the base of the mountain. He hacks a little tunnel right through the mountain. He leaves the coach standing, and on with him at a run after the princess.

The billy goat was scampering, scampering. The princess spoke out of the bundle of hay:

> *'Little billy goat, little billy goat,*
> *Do I hear the sound of footsteps?*
> *Stoop your ear to the ground and listen –*
> *Is that the demon running behind us?'*

The billy goat stooped his ear to the ground and said:

> *'He comes, he comes, he comes*
> *Like a whirlwind he comes,*
> *He is already near.'*

'Billy goat, billy goat, what shall I do?'

And the billy goat said, 'Feel in my right ear. You will find a tinder box. Throw it behind you.'

The princess took the tinder box out of the billy goat's right ear, and threw it behind her, saying:

> *'May you become a flaming river,*
> *A flaming river behind me.*
> *No bird to fly over it,*
> *No beast to swim over it,*
> *The demon not to get through it.'*

And there behind the princess flowed a river of flame. But the billy goat said:

> *'Princess, princess, I am weary with running,*
> *My little back aches,*
> *My little legs ache,*
> *My little head aches,*
> *I must rest before I go farther.'*

'Then we will stay here and rest awhile,' said the princess. 'The demon will never cross that flaming river.'

Oh, wouldn't he? The flaming river wasn't very broad. The demon thought, 'If I had a pole to help me, my long legs would jump it.'

So he ran to a tree that was growing near the river, drew his sword, hacked, hacked, and cut off a long, straight branch.

And the princess cried out:

> *'Billy goat, billy goat,*
> *Look at the demon!*
> *He is taking a pole to jump over the river!*
> *If your tired little legs won't run any farther,*
> *Alas, my billy goat, what shall we do?'*

And the billy goat answered, 'Throw a stick into the river.'
So the princess took a stick, threw it into the river, and said:

> *'May this stick become a bridge,*
> *A bridge for me to cross back over the river,*
> *A high curved bridge that folds itself up*
> *And vanishes behind me.'*

Then the stick became a bridge, curving high above the flames of the river. And the billy goat stepped on to the bridge, carrying the princess.

The demon had made his jumping pole, he had planted it deep in the river, he had taken his flying leap, and landed on the far bank. The pole had slipped from his hand and dropped into the river. No matter, there he was safe on the bank! But when he saw the billy goat walking wearily back over the bridge with the princess, he roared with rage, and rushed to jump on to the bridge himself.

But, lo, the bridge was folding itself up and vanishing behind the princess. And when the demon tried to jump on to it – where did he land?

Slap! Into the flaming river. And that was the end of him.

'We needn't hurry ourselves now,' said the billy goat.

The princess slid from his back and brushed herself clean of hay.

'No, indeed we needn't hurry,' she said. 'My little darling billy goat, you have saved my life!' And she took the billy goat's head between her hands and kissed it.

Oh! oh! oh! The billy goat has vanished. And there in front of the princess stands a handsome, smiling prince.

'Oh, oh, oh! Who are *you*?'

'I am your billy goat,' said the handsome, smiling prince. 'Your billy goat whom long ago a jealous fairy put under a spell. But your kiss has broken the spell. I love you dearly, little princess. Will you take me for your husband?'

'Of course I will!' said the princess.

So hand in hand they walked leisurely back to the palace. And if it was a long way, it didn't seem long to them.

The king was very surprised to see the prince. But the queen said, 'I knew I could trust my billy goat to do the right thing – and the wedding feast is still waiting.'

So the prince and princess were married. And they all lived happily ever after.

4 · The Wizard King

Once upon a time there was a wizard king who ruled over a country as flat as a tablecloth. This king delighted in playing tricks, and his tricks weren't always kind ones.

So one day the king held a banquet in his white stone palace, for any of his people who cared to come. And a crowd came. And in the middle of the banquet the king got up and said, 'My people, I seek a husband for the princess, my daughter; but that husband must be as clever as I am. If there is any man here who can succeed in hiding himself from me – why then, that man shall have the princess to wife and half my kingdom also. But if he does not succeed, he shall lose his head.'

The guests were silent; they turned pale. What trick would their wizard king be up to next?

But there was a bold bright boy among the guests. He looked across the table at the princess: she was very lovely. So he stands up and says, 'Sire, *I* will hide from you!'

The wizard king laughs. 'Be off with you then, my bold bright boy. I will look for you tomorrow morning . . . And you shall give me your head.'

The bold bright boy went from the palace. He went through the streets of the city, he went, went, went, till he came to a bath house.

'Ah ha!' thinks he. 'This is where I will hide!'

And he tiptoes into the bath house, and hides under a bench in the corner.

In his white stone palace the wizard king slept through the night. Early in the morning he rose, bathed himself in well water, lit a fire

40

in his magic brazier, took his magic book, sat in his ivory chair, opened his magic book and began to read: 'The bold bright boy has left my white stone hall. He has gone through the streets of the city as far as the bath house. And in his mind he is thinking "Where shall I flee and hide from the king? I will go into the bath house and creep under a bench in the corner . . ." '

'Go, my servants; bring that boy to me.'

The servants go to the bath house. They lift up the bench. There is the boy.

'Good morning, bold bright boy!'

'Good morning, king's servants.'

'Come, bright boy, the king has called you to himself.'

And they brought the boy to the king.

'Good morning, my bold bright boy.'

'Good morning, my lord the king.'

'Are you ready to lose your head, my bold bright boy?'

'Since I can no other.'

'Pish!' said the king. 'What use is your foolish head to me?' And he bade his servants whip the boy soundly and let him go home.

Again the king gave a banquet; again he promised his daughter to any man who was clever enough to hide from him; and again the one who tried to hide and didn't succeed was to lose his head. Again the guests were silent and turned pale, until a tall handsome lad, seeing how lovely the princess was, stood up and said, 'Sire, I will hide.'

The wizard king laughs. 'Be off with you then, my tall handsome lad. I will look for you tomorrow morning . . . And you shall give me your head.'

The tall handsome lad went from the palace. He went through the streets of the city, he went, went, went, till he came to a great barn filled with hay. Thinks he, 'I will creep into the hay and hide. How shall the king find me?' And into the barn he goes, covers himself over with hay, and lies still.

In his white stone palace the king slept through the night. Early in the morning he rose, bathed himself in well water, lit a fire in his magic brazier, took his magic book, sat in his ivory chair, opened his magic book, and read: 'The tall handsome lad has left my white stone hall. He has gone through the streets of the city as far as the great barn filled with hay. And in his mind he thought, "Where shall I hide from the king? I will go into the barn and creep under the hay . . ." '

'Go, my servants; bring that lad to me.'

And the servants brought him.

'Good morning, my tall handsome lad.'

'Good morning, my lord the king.'

'Are you ready to lose your head?'

'Since I can no other.'

'Pish!' said the king. 'What use to me is a head without brains?' And he bade his servants whip the lad soundly, and let him go home.

The king went about chuckling. He wasn't in a hurry to find a

husband for his daughter. But it pleased him to show his people how clever he was. So he held yet a third banquet; and the people crowded to it by the king's orders though some would rather have stayed away.

Now it so happened that a prince from a neighbouring kingdom had seen a portrait of the princess, and having fallen in love with her lovely face, had set out to ask for her hand. He arrived at the king's palace just as the guests were sitting down to the banquet, and he took his place among them. So when again the king challenged any of the guests to hide from him, the prince stood up and said, 'I will hide, but only on one condition.'

'And who are you to make conditions?' said the king.

'Sire, I am Prince Ladislov, at your service.'

'Oh ho, Prince Ladislov, and what is the condition?'

'That you will give me not only one chance, but three.'

The king said, 'I will give you three chances. But there will be no letting you off with a whipping if you fail. Prince or no prince, I will have your head!'

The prince said, 'I do not intend to fail.'

He looked across the table at the princess; the princess looked across the table at him. Oh, but she was beautiful, and oh, but he was handsome! And the princess thought, 'Pray heaven he does not fail!'

And what made Prince Ladislov so confident that he wouldn't fail? Just this: he knew some magic himself, having a magician for a godfather. So he went out of the white stone palace into the streets of the city and along and along till he came to the open country. Then he turned himself into a stoat with a black tail.

The stoat ran, ran, ran; he crept under every stone and every heap of wood; he twisted and turned, climbing over walls, pushing through hedges; and so, having confused his tracks, came in a wide circle back to the white stone palace. There the stoat turned into a little golden beetle, and the little golden beetle went dancing, dancing under the palace windows till he found the window of the princess's room, and it was open. So the little golden beetle turned into a bright falcon, and hopped on to the window sill.

'Oh, lovely bird, lovely bird, come to me!' cried the princess.

And the bright falcon hopped down on to the floor, and turned into the prince.

Well, there: prince and princess chat together all through the night, and by dawn they have plighted their troth. Then the prince turns into a gold ring, the princess puts the ring on her finger, and goes to bed.

Meanwhile the wizard king had slept through the night. Early in the morning he rose, washed himself in well water, lit a fire in his magic brazier, took his magic book, sat in his ivory chair, opened the magic book and read. And when he had done reading, he said to his servants, 'Go, bring the princess to me,'

The servants went. But the princess said, 'I am not well. I cannot rise from my bed.'

The servants told the king. The king said 'Pish!' went to the princess's room and said, 'Give me the gold ring you are wearing.'

The princess didn't want to give the ring to the king, but he made her. Then the king threw the ring over his left shoulder, and it turned into Prince Ladislov.

The king said, 'Good day, prince!'

The prince said, 'Good day, sire!'

The king said, 'Are you ready to lose your head?'

The prince said, 'No, I am not ready. Have you forgotten our agreement?'

The king said, 'Bother the agreement! Oh, all right, be off with you! But wherever you hide, I shall find you.'

'That's as may be,' said the prince.

The prince went out of the white stone palace. He went, went, went through the streets of the city and out into the open country. There he turned himself into a grey wolf, and the grey wolf ran and leaped, ran and leaped over miles and miles till he came to a dark wood.

Then the grey wolf turned himself into a bear, and the bear trudged, trudged, trudged mile after mile, came out of the wood and turned himself into a stoat with a black tail. The stoat went, went, went, till he came to a meadow edged with dykes and willows. And there the stoat turned himself into seventy-seven grass blades; and the seventy-seven grass blades joined themselves together and became a single blade.

The wizard king slept through the night. Early in the morning he rose, bathed himself in well water, lit a fire in his magic brazier, sat in his ivory chair, opened his magic book, and read: 'Ah ha, prince, ah ha, grey wolf, ah ha, bear, ah ha, stoat with the black tail! Every step you have taken, every twist and turn you have made – there it is, all plain to see in the king's magic book. Ah ha, seventy-seven grass blades; and ah ha, single grass blade – the king knows all about you!'

And the king said to his servants, 'Ride out into the country; ride, ride, till you come to a meadow edged about with dykes and willows. From each kind of grass in the meadow tear up an armful, and bring all those armfuls to me.'

The servants did as the king bade them. They came back with armfuls of grass, and heaped the grass before the king. The king sat in his ivory chair; he searched through the heaps of grass blade by blade. He found the blade he sought, threw it over his left shoulder.

There stands the prince.

'Good morning, Prince Ladislov!'

'Good morning, my liege!'

'Are you ready to lose your head?'

'No, I am not ready. Have you forgotten our agreement?'

'Bother the agreement! Oh, all right – be off with you for the last time! But wherever you hide, I shall find you.'

'That's as may be.'

The prince went out of the white stone palace; he went, went, went through the streets of the city, and out into the open country.

45

There he turned into a grey wolf, and the grey wolf ran and leaped, ran and leaped till he came to the blue sea. Then the grey wolf turned into a silver pike. The silver pike sprang into the water, and swam, swam, swam through the blue sea till he came to a yellow beach. Then the silver pike turned into a bright falcon. The bright falcon flew, flew, flew till he came to a great oak tree. At the top of the oak tree was the nest of the big bird Magowitch. And the bright falcon dropped into the nest.

But the big bird Magowitch comes flying back to his nest and sees the bright falcon.

'Ah, what a churl, to fly into a strange nest and lie down!'

And the big bird Magowitch makes to snatch the bright falcon in his talons to tear him to pieces. But down out of the high clouds swoops an eagle. And the eagle drives the big bird Magowitch from the tree.

And the eagle spoke, and the prince knew him. It was the magician, his godfather.

Said the eagle, 'How now, my son! Have I taught you magic to no better purpose than to race about the world in this shape and that shape? Is not every shape you take, and every twist and turn you make, plainly to be read by the wizard king in his book of magic? Have you yet to learn, my son, that *it is only on a page where nothing is written that nothing can be read?*'

And the eagle smote the bright falcon and said, 'Become a blank page in the wizard king's magic book.'

And lo! The bright falcon vanished, and the eagle vanished . . .

In his white stone palace the wizard king slept through the night. Early in the morning he rose, washed himself in well water, lit his magic brazier, sat in his ivory chair, opened his magic book and read: 'Prince Ladislov has left my white stone hall. He has gone through the streets of the city and out into the open country. He has turned himself into a grey wolf. The grey wolf has leaped and run, leaped and run till he comes to the blue sea. There he has turned himself into a silver pike. The silver pike has swum through the blue sea to a yellow beach. There the silver pike has turned into a bright falcon. The bright falcon has flown, flown, flown till he comes to the great oak tree where big bird Magowitch has his nest. The bright falcon has dropped into that nest . . .'

The wizard king turned the page of his magic book. There was no more written in the book. The next page was blank.

And the wizard king said to his servants, 'Ride out into the country, ride, ride, ride till you come to the blue sea. Cross the blue sea in the boat you will find waiting. Land on the yellow beach; ride, ride, ride, till you come to the great oak tree where the big bird Magowitch has his nest. Climb the tree, look in the nest; there you will find a bright falcon. Bring that falcon to me.'

The servants set out; they rode, rode, rode; they crossed the blue sea, they landed on the yellow beach; they rode, rode, rode, till they came to the great oak tree; they climbed the oak tree and looked in the nest.

But the nest was empty. So they came back to the wizard king.

'Sire, the nest of the big bird Magowitch is empty.'

The wizard king reads again in his magic book. 'Fools, dolts, imbeciles, *Prince Ladislov is in that nest!*'

'Sire, we could not see him.'

'Then I must go myself!' cries the wizard king. And he sets out with his servants.

They come to the great oak tree. The wizard king climbs the tree, looks in the nest. Empty! In a great rage he orders his servants to cut down the tree, to chop it into small splinters, to set fire to those splinters, to burn, burn, burn, till nothing is left but a heap of ashes.

'And even if I haven't found the prince,' says he, as he goes back to his white stone palace, 'the rascal is not living any longer. And he has saved me the trouble of cutting off his head.'

So three days go by. And then, one morning, as the wizard king sits in his ivory chair, reading in his magic book, a blank page of the book gives a jump over the king's left shoulder, lands on the floor, and turns into Prince Ladislov.

'Good day, king!'

'Good day, prince! So I must chop off your head after all!'

'Not so, king! You sought me: you could not find me. Now I have come back of my own accord to claim what you have promised: the princess and half the kingdom.'

What could the wizard king do? He was beaten, and he knew it. So he held a grand wedding for Prince Ladislov and the princess, and gave a great feast to all his people. But he sulked at the feast and made no speech at all.

And at the end of the feast the prince stood up and said to the wizard king, 'You can keep your half kingdom, I don't want it. My own country is prettier; it is not as flat as a tablecloth, and in it we live happily; we don't play unkind tricks on people.'

So Prince Ladislov took the princess home to his own country, where they lived happy and contented. And may we live as happily!

5 · The Enchanted Prince

There was a king whose dreams came true. And his queen had a baby son. And the king dreamed that if the child's feet touched the ground before he was twelve years old, something dreadful would happen to him. So the little prince was never allowed to walk.

First he was carried about by his nurse; then, as he grew older, he drove in a little carriage, with a page to lift him out of his chair into the carriage, and out of the carriage into his chair again. And when he was a little older still, he rode on a pony; and the page lifted him on to the pony when he set out, and lifted him off the pony when he came home.

All went well with the little prince; he was handsome, he was clever, he was good, and everybody loved him.

So when the time of the prince's twelfth birthday drew near, the king prepared a great feast of thanksgiving; and the queen said, 'Tomorrow, my dear little son, you shall walk and run and play in the garden like other children!' And the little prince was very, very happy.

So on that day, the day before his twelfth birthday, a groom brought round the prince's pony for him to go a-riding; and a page carried the prince out into the courtyard to lift him on to the pony's back.

The prince has one foot in the stirrup; he waves to the queen who is watching from a window; he is laughing to think how tomorrow he will walk and run, when suddenly the sky grows dark, there comes a clap of thunder, with echoing sounds terrible to hear – screams and groans and howlings. The palace shakes, the earth

49

trembles, the pony rears up in fright, the page lets go his hold, the little prince slithers off the pony's back. And his feet touch the ground.

Immediately all is quiet again. But where is the prince? The prince has vanished.

What grief! What horror! The queen has fainted, the king is weeping, everyone in the palace is running up and down, searching, searching, searching. It is all in vain. The whole kingdom is searched, a big reward is offered for the finding of the prince. But the prince is not found.

Years passed. Every year on the prince's birthday the queen put on mourning. 'Now my darling would be thirteen,' she said, 'now fourteen, now fifteen, now sixteen, seventeen, eighteen.' And every year she made a beautiful suit of clothes to fit the prince who never came back to her. The clothes hung in the wardrobe year after year; they glistened with the queen's tears; it was all very, very sad.

Now in the palace there was a beautiful room that had been prepared for the prince to sleep in on his twelfth birthday. So in the year when the prince would have been eighteen, the man who had been the prince's page, going late to bed, passed the door of this room at midnight.

'Poor little prince!' thinks he, and stops a moment by the door. And as he so stood, thinking of the prince, he heard from within the room the sound of footsteps. And not only footsteps, but sighs and groans.

The man pushed the door open and peeped into the room. What did he see? He saw the moonlight shining in through the window, but he saw nothing else. The room was empty. And yet the footsteps passed over the floor, and the sighs and groans were in his ears. Terrified, he pulled the door shut again, fled to his bed, and put his head under the clothes.

In the morning the man told the king. And the next midnight both the king and the queen went to the room. Yes, they heard the footsteps, they heard the sighs, they heard the groans, but they saw no one. And so it went on, midnight after midnight, and every one knew that the room was haunted.

And the king dreamed again. He dreamed of a voice. The voice said, 'Your son is spellbound in that room. If a maiden will watch in the room all night, it may be that she can break the spell. But only if she is the right maiden.'

So then the king, having faith in his dream, offered three hundred pieces of gold to any unmarried girl who would watch in the room all night.

The girls were not backward. Many and many a one agreed to watch. But when at midnight came the footsteps and the sighs and the groans of the unseen presence, every girl took fright and fled. Even the promise of three hundred pieces of gold wouldn't tempt any of them to enter that room again.

Now there lived not far from the palace a widow with three daughters. The widow owned a little mill, and by grinding corn for the neighbours she just managed to make a living. But the girls had to be content with poor fare and shabby clothes. Three hundred pieces of gold seemed like a fortune to them, you may be sure.

'Three hundred pieces of gold!' sighed the eldest daughter. 'For three hundred pieces of gold I would sup with the Devil himself!'

And she went to her mother and said, 'Mother, tonight I will watch in the prince's room.'

The mother said, 'If you are not afraid – go!'

So the girl went to the king. She asked for food to cook for her supper, some dry wood to light a fire, a cooking-pot, and a lantern, and assured the king that she wouldn't come out of the room till morning.

Well, she gets the things she asks for, and goes to the room. She lights a fire, puts the food in the cooking-pot, and the cooking-pot on the fire, lays the table, makes the bed. She is busy till midnight, and just when the food is about cooked, and the table nicely laid, there comes the sound of light footsteps moving about the room, and now a sigh, and now a groan, and now another sigh.

You may be sure the girl is scared, but she puts a bold face on it, and cries out, 'Who are you? Where are you? Why don't you show yourself?' She runs about searching, she peeps in the wardrobe, she looks behind the curtains, under the table – no one! She gets on her hands and knees to look under the bed, and – would you believe it? – when she straightens herself up again, there is a young man standing at her side.

The young man was wearing a suit of clothes made by the queen's own hands: doublet and hose of silk, an embroidered cloak, and on his head a narrow gold coronet where one great ruby glowed. Surely it is the prince himself! But oh, what a sad, sad face!

And the prince spoke and said, 'For whom are you cooking?'

Says she, 'For myself alone.'

Says he, 'And for whom is the table spread?'

Says she, 'For myself alone.'

Says he, 'And the bed – for whom is it made?'

Says she, 'For myself – who else?'

Ah me! The prince is shedding tears. One moment he is there, wringing his hands and weeping, the next moment he has gone.

And the sound of footsteps ceased; nor were the sighs and groans heard any more.

So the girl ate her supper and went to bed.

In the morning the girl went to the king and said, 'I stayed in the room all night.'

And she told him what she had seen.

'You cannot be the right maiden,' said the king sadly.

And he gave her the three hundred gold pieces, and sent her home.

When the widow's second daughter saw the gold pieces, she said, 'Tonight *I* will watch!' And watch she did, doing just what her sister had done. She lit a fire in the room, put on her supper to cook, laid the table, made the bed. At midnight she heard the footsteps, the sighs, the groans. The prince appeared, asked her the same questions, got the same answers, wrung his hands, wept, and vanished. But the girl stayed in the room all night, and got the three hundred gold pieces from the king in the morning. And that was all she cared about.

'Poor prince!' said the widow's youngest daughter. And she went to her mother.

'Mother, let me watch in the prince's room tonight.'

'No, no,' said the widow, 'you are too young, you would be badly frightened. Though I own we could do with three hundred more pieces of gold.'

'It's not that,' said the girl. 'I would like to set him free.'

'Set him free indeed!' said the eldest sister. 'That's foolish talk! As long as the prince stays where he is, won't there be gold pieces for the taking? Now, listen to me!'

And she told the youngest sister exactly what the prince would say, and how she was to answer him. 'You say just what I said, and he'll go away. You'll have a peaceful night of it, and get your gold in the morning.'

The youngest sister said again, 'Mother, let me go!'

'Well then – go!' said the widow, thinking of the gold.

So the youngest sister went to the palace and told the king she would like to watch. The king sighed. He was giving up hope. But he let the girl have the things she asked for: a lantern, dry sticks to light a fire, food for her supper, and a cooking-pot.

And the girl went to the room.

She lit the fire, put on her supper to cook, laid the table, made the bed, sat down and waited. At midnight came the footsteps, the sighs, the groans. The girl's heart beat fast, but she sat quiet as a mouse. And all at once, there was the prince, standing in front of her. How sad, how sad, he looked!

Said he, 'For whom are you cooking?'

The girl didn't answer. Her sister had told her what she must say, but somehow she couldn't say it: it seemed too unkind.

The prince frowned. Then he said again, still more sadly, 'Will you not tell me – for whom are you cooking?'

'I was cooking for myself,' answered the girl. 'But if you will –
for you also.' And when she said that, the prince smiled.

'And the table – for whom is it laid?'

'For myself,' said she. 'Unless you would wish to sit there also?'

The prince didn't look sad any more, he looked quite joyful.
'And for whom is the bed made?'

'I made it for myself,' answered the girl. 'But you can sleep there
if you wish.'

The prince clapped his hands. 'Ah, what happiness! I accept, I
accept both supper and bed! But wait – first I must thank those
who have been good to me.'

Then a sweet, moist breeze, smelling of springtime, blew
through the room, and the floor opened. Under the floor was a
deep, dark precipice, going down and down. The prince stepped
down into the precipice. The girl stepped down after him. She
was not walking, she was slowly falling, down and down and down.
It was very dark and frightening, but she didn't wish to turn back,
nor could she have turned back had she wanted to.

And then, all at once, she was in a new world. To her right

hand flowed a river of liquid gold. To her left hand shone the crests of golden mountains. And between the river and the mountains was a vast meadow with green lawns and thousands of flower beds. The prince was walking among the flower beds; the girl followed. He didn't turn round. He didn't seem to know she was there. He stooped and talked to the flowers, hailed them as old friends, and kissed them. The flowers nodded back to the prince; the girl knew they were talking to him, though she couldn't hear what they were saying.

The prince walked on, the girl followed; not once did the prince look round. He came to a forest where all the trees were gold, and where innumerable birds sang among the branches. The birds hovered about the prince, singing their sweetest songs, and perching on his shoulders. The prince walked on and on, talking to the birds, caressing them. The girl followed the prince; she broke off a golden branch and hid it under her apron.

They passed through the forest of gold trees, and came to another forest, where the trees were silver, and where innumerable animals came running from among the trees to greet the prince. The prince talked to the animals, thanked them, caressed them, bade them goodbye. The girl, following, broke off a silver branch and hid it under her apron.

'Farewell! Farewell!' said the prince to the animals. And he turned and went back through the silver wood and into the gold one. 'Farewell! Farewell!' he said to the birds, and passed out of the gold forest into the meadow. 'Farewell! Farewell!' he said to the flowers; and there he was back at the bottom of the precipice, and the girl was behind him. And all this time he had not once looked at her. But now he began floating up the precipice, and the girl caught the end of his cloak and floated up after him. And still he did not notice her.

Not until they were back in the room, and the hole in the floor had closed behind them, did the prince look at the girl. And then he smiled and said, 'My farewells are made. Now we can sup.'

And they sat down to supper. By and by the prince drew his hand across his eyes and said, 'Our hunger is satisfied. Now we can sleep.' And he went and lay down on the bed, and fell asleep.

The girl took the gold branch and the silver branch from under her apron. She put the gold branch at the prince's head, and the silver branch at his feet. And when she had done that, she sat down by the fire and watched till dawn. Then she, too, fell asleep.

In the morning the king waited impatiently for the girl to come and tell him how she had fared. But the girl didn't come. The king waited and waited: the sun was well up, and still the girl didn't come. What could have happened? The king felt anxious. He went to the room – opened the door. What did he see?

He saw the prince, his son, asleep on the bed, and the girl asleep by the fire.

'My son! My son!' The king danced for joy. He rushed from the room and called the queen, the courtiers, the lords in waiting, the ladies in waiting – every one. 'Come and see! Come and see!' They came crowding into the room; their joyful cries woke the prince, woke the girl. The prince looked at the two branches: the gold branch at his head, the silver branch at his feet. He looked at the girl. 'You followed me! You were not afraid?'

'I was sore afraid,' said the girl. 'But I followed you.'

'And you have broken the spell and delivered me!' said the prince. 'Now you shall never leave me! You shall be my bride, and these two branches shall be our palaces.'

Then the prince picked up the gold branch and the silver branch and tossed them out of the window.

And where those two branches fell to earth, there rose up two splendid palaces: the one pure gold, the other pure silver.

So at last the king was able to give his great feast of thanksgiving, and the prince and the girl were married. Sometimes they lived in their silver palace, and sometimes they lived in their golden one. But whichever palace they lived in, they lived happily.

6 · *The Magic Belt*

There was a king who took ship and went to sea with his queen and his little son, John. But the ship struck a rock and foundered: king, queen, little prince, and sailors were all thrown into the waves. The waves tossed them here, tossed them there, snatched them away one from the other, and little prince John was thrown up on a rocky shore.

So there he was, cold, miserable, drenched to the skin, and all alone. But he was a brave little fellow, and though he cried at first, he cheered up by and by. The hot sun dried his clothes, and the hot sun made him feel very sleepy; so he lay down on some sweet-smelling grass close to the shore, shut his eyes, and fell asleep.

When he woke up it was night; the moon was shining, and some-one was calling him:

'Little Prince John, get up, little rascal!'

Little Prince John scrambled to his feet and rubbed his eyes. A big man was bending over him, and the big man was carrying a boat, no bigger than a shoe, tucked under his arm.

'Oh, who are *you*, and what is your name?' asked little Prince John.

'My-Name-is-my-Name,' said the big man. 'Are you hungry?'

'Yes, I am,' said little Prince John.

The big man snapped his fingers, and there on the grass appeared a fine meal: bread, meat, cake, and a cup of milk.

Did little Prince John eat? I tell you he did! He ate and ate till there was nothing left, and the big man laughed to see him.

And when he had eaten his fill, little Prince John, who was

always polite, bowed to the big man and said, 'I am very much obliged to you, sir.'

'Now we will go fishing,' said My-Name-is-my-Name; and he went down to the edge of the sea, and little Prince John followed him.

'But where is the boat that we are to go fishing in?' asked little Prince John.

'Here under my arm,' said My-Name-is-my-Name. And he set the tiny boat on the water, and it became a big boat.

So they both get into the boat. Away over the water it goes, without sail, without oars, without rudder. And the fish they caught, you wouldn't believe; though how they caught them I can't tell you, for they had neither net, nor line, nor any other gear.

By and by the boat took them to shore again, and when they had landed, that boat became tiny again, and My-Name-is-my-Name tucked it under his arm. And all the fish they had caught he put in his pocket, for the fish had grown small as well.

'Now follow me,' said My-Name-is-my-Name, 'for where I live, you shall live, and I will take care of you.' And he led little Prince John along the shore till they came to a big cave. And when they

went into the cave, little Prince John was more than astonished, for it was all lit up and full of fairies.

Prince John lived with the fairies and went fishing with My-Name-is-my-Name for seven whole years, though the time seemed to him but seven days. Only, whereas he had been a little lad when he first went into the cave, now he was a big lad: tall, strong and handsome.

So one day he said, 'Master, I would now like to leave you, and go out into the world.'

'You had better stay with us,' said My-Name-is-my-Name. 'The world is full of trouble.'

'Yet I would go into the world, Master.'

'Then I can't keep you,' said My-Name-is-my-Name. 'But before you go, I have a gift for you. Here is a magic belt. Put it round your waist under your clothes, and wear it always. Tell no man of it, let no man see it, or it will lose its virtue. All that you ask of it, it will give you. You will be able to go on the sea or under the sea, on the earth or under the earth, according to your wish. And each time you desire anything, you have but to ask it.'

'This is indeed a precious gift,' said the young Prince John. 'And I thank you with all my heart, Master.' So he fastened the belt round his waist under his shirt, took a graceful leave of My-Name-is-my-Name, and set out into the world.

He walked, walked, and by and by he came to a city with a harbour and many ships. And seeing a big ship about to set sail, he took service in her as a cabin boy. But they hadn't been long at sea when he discovered that captain and crew were pirates. Many a gallant ship did they scuttle, many a brave sailor did they make walk the plank, and many rich cargoes of merchandise did they seize for their rascally selves.

'Ah! If I were but on land again I would denounce you all!' cried young Prince John.

The captain scowled and took counsel with his crew.

'We must get rid of that cabin boy,' says he.

'Hang him!' says one.

'Chop off his head!' says another.

'No, no,' says a third, less brutal than the rest. 'Here is a big empty cask. Let us put the lad into the cask and throw it into the sea.'

So that's what they did; and this third sailor, when no one was looking, put into the cask a loaf of bread and a bottle of water. And then, heave ho! Overboard went the cask and young Prince John.

The cask floated away on the top of the waves. And Prince John said to himself, 'The sea is full of ships. Maybe I shall meet with one and still save myself; or maybe the waves will toss me up on some distant shore. I must make my bread and water last as long as I can.'

So each day he nibbled only a small piece of bread, and drank only a few drops of water. And he had already been many days in the cask when he suddenly remembered the belt he was wearing.

'Well, what a blockhead I am!' thinks he. 'Now we will see if this belt of mine is really magic! Magic belt, magic belt, carry me to port. And let that port be the one the pirate ship is making for, that I may denounce these men and put a stop to their wickedness.'

And no sooner had he spoken than there came a following wind, and the wind carried the cask in the wake of the pirate ship.

The pirate ship sailed on, the cask followed in its wake; and young Prince John, who had now no bread left, and whose water bottle was empty, said, 'Magic belt, magic belt, give me to eat and drink.'

Hey presto! There in the cask is food in plenty – meat and bread, cake and wine.

'Oh, my treasure of a belt!' cried young Prince John. And he blessed the giver of the belt with a grateful heart.

At the end of two or three days he looked out from his cask, and saw before him the roofs and walls of a port, with a harbour full of vessels, big and small, and among them the pirate ship moored alongside the quay. 'Magic belt, magic belt,' said he, 'let my cask be now submerged, that the pirates may not see me.'

Hey presto! There is the cask, floating along the bottom of the sea.

But before it submerged the pirate captain had seen it, and he said to his mate, 'Surely that was the cask we threw overboard with the cabin boy?'

'Yes, yes,' says the mate, 'I recognise it.'

'We must try and catch it,' says the captain. 'For if that wicked cabin boy is still alive, he will surely denounce us as he threatened.'

And he sent out a rowing boat to search for the cask.

But young Prince John said, 'Magic belt, magic belt, bring my cask to shore out of sight of the harbour.'

And a wave lifted the cask, swept it away from the harbour, and brought it to shore under a green where people were walking. The wave ran back: there was the cask, high and dry. Young Prince John stepped out of it. 'Bring me to your king,' said he to the people who ran to greet him.

So they brought him to the king; and young Prince John told the king about the pirates. The king sent his soldiers to the pirate ship; he had the pirates brought before him in chains and condemned them to death. But young Prince John said, 'I would crave the life of the pirate who had pity on me.'

So the king spared the life of this one pirate.

And when all was done, and the crowds who had gathered about the king's palace had gone home, the king said to young Prince John, 'Cabin boy, do you know what the people have been saying about you? They have been saying that you, who followed the pirate ship across the sea in a cask, must be a miracle-worker. Cabin boy, I am in great sorrow, and it may be that you can help me. Know then that I once had two beautiful daughters, but a demon has stolen them from me. The demon keeps my poor dear daughters prisoners in a castle on a rock at the mouth of a river far across the sea. And oh me, alas, he has changed them both into monkeys. The rock is guarded by such fierce beasts that no man can approach it. I have sent ship after ship after ship, and gallant men enough to the island; but all who have tried to land there have perished. Yes, even their ships have been swallowed down by those fierce beasts. Cabin boy, cabin boy, if you are indeed a miracle-worker, can you not bring my daughters back to me?'

'Sire,' said young Prince John, 'I will do my best. Make me a cask, as big a cask as you are able, with staves of transparent horn at the two ends, so that my cask may be lighted. And let there be a panel on the top of the cask that will open and shut, and yet be watertight.'

The king sent for the best coopers in the town, and bade them make such a cask; and when it was ready, and well stocked with food and drink, young Prince John had it rolled down to the harbour and put into the sea. Then he stepped into it, waved his hand to the crowds that had gathered on the quay to watch him embark, and closed the sliding panel over his head.

'Magic belt, magic belt,' said he, 'let my cask carry me to the castle where the princesses are held captive.'

Away rushed the cask over the water; the people on the quay had scarcely time to raise a cheer before the cask was out of sight. And on and on that cask sped over the water, until, after several days, Prince John said, 'Magic belt, magic belt, if I am soon to reach the castle, let my cask travel under water.'

And the magic belt spoke up and said, 'We have still twenty-four hours' more sailing.'

'Nevertheless,' said Prince John, 'let my cask travel under the water, lest the fierce beasts smell me from afar.'

The cask sank down and sped along the bottom of the sea; and so came to the mouth of a great river. There, on a black rock in the midst of the river, stood a mighty castle; and even under the sea, in his closed cask, Prince John could hear the roarings of the beasts that guarded it.

'Magic belt, magic belt,' said he, 'let there be a tunnel driven under the water through this rock, and let the cask travel through that tunnel until it brings me beneath the room where I shall find the princesses.'

And the tunnel opened itself, and the cask rushed through it in the darkness, and brought Prince John safely under the room of the princesses. And there it stopped.

So Prince John stepped out of the cask, ran up some stone stairs, pushed open a door at the top of the stairs, and came into an arched room. And in that room sat two big monkeys, the one white, the other black.

The monkeys had their heads buried in their hands; they looked very miserable, but when they saw Prince John they leaped to their feet.

'Who are you?' cried the white monkey.

'I am Prince John.'

'And I am the princess Peerless Flower,' said the white monkey, 'and this is my sister, Goodness Unparalleled. How did you come here, where no one comes? But however you came, get you gone, get you gone, before the wild beasts scent you out and devour you!'

'Ah no, I am come to set you free.'

'Alas, alas, you cannot do that,' said the black monkey.

'I can and I will. Follow me.' And Prince John led the two monkeys out of the room and down the stone stairs to where the cask floated in the tunnel.

They all three got into the cask. Prince John closed the sliding panel and said, 'Magic belt, magic belt, let this cask carry us back under the water into the open sea.'

Away whizzed the cask through the tunnel and out into the open sea; and away with it then across the ocean along the sea bed. And as it went, the roarings of the fierce beasts that guarded the castle grew fainter and fainter, and died into silence.

Then Prince John said, 'Magic belt, magic belt, let the cask rise to the surface of the water.'

Immediately the cask rose, and Prince John said, 'Magic belt, let the cask carry the princesses back to the king, their father.'

And the cask sped over the water faster than any wind that blows.

Now since Prince John had set out, the king, the princesses' father, had put sentries on the roof of his palace to watch the sea for the return of the cask. And when at last the sentries saw the cask speeding over the waves and drawing nearer and nearer, they rushed to tell the king.

'And has he brought my daughters?' cried the king.

'Ah, your majesty, that we do not know. But the panel on the top of the cask is open and there is a flag flying from it.'

'Bring me a spy-glass!' cried the king, and he hurried up on to the palace roof. Yes, with his spy-glass the king saw the cask distinctly; and he saw, too, a pole thrust through the open panel, he saw a flag flying from the pole, and he saw that there were words written on the flag. And as the cask came nearer and nearer the king was able to read those words. And the words said, I HAVE THE TWO PRINCESSES.

Then – what rejoicing, what firing of cannon, what rushing down to the harbour of all the people in the town!

But when the cask drew in at the quay, and Prince John stepped out of it, what should he be leading in either hand but a large monkey, the one white, the other black.

'My daughters, my poor, poor daughters!' cried the king, and burst into tears.

But Prince John said, 'Magic belt, magic belt, let the spell which is upon the two princesses be lifted.'

And hey presto! The monkeys vanish, and two beautiful princesses run to embrace their father.

'Cabin boy, cabin boy,' cried the king, 'ask what you will! My kingdom, my wealth, all that I have is yours!'

The prince laughed. 'No need to call me "cabin boy" any longer. I am a prince, and my name is John.'

'Then here and now I make you my heir,' said the king, 'and I give you one of my daughters in marriage. Choose which you will.'

Prince John looked from one princess to the other: both so beautiful, but Peerless Flower more beautiful than her sister. Should Peerless Flower then be his bride? Ah no! 'For the beauty of a flower may perish with the years,' he thought, 'but goodness never.' And he took Goodness Unparalleled by the hand and said, 'You are my choice – if you are willing?'

'Yes, I am willing,' said she.

So they were married. Prince John became the king's heir, and in course of time became king himself. He ruled wisely, never ceasing to be grateful to My-Name-is-my-Name for the gift of the magic belt. But he couldn't keep a secret from his lovely wife. One day he showed Goodness Unparalleled the magic belt; and then, as My-Name-is-my-Name had warned him, the belt lost its virtue. It was nothing now but a little scrap of woven silk.

What matter? Our John was so happy that it seemed he had nothing left to wish for.

7 · *The Prince and the Dragons*

An emperor had three sons, and the eldest rode out hunting. And he had just passed through the city gates when a hare jumped out of a bush. Off goes the hare, off goes the prince after it, this way, that way, over hill, over dale, till they come to a watermill. In through the open door of the mill darts the hare; in through the open door thinks the prince to go after it: when, lo! Out of the mill comes a dragoness. That dragoness pulled the prince off his horse. The horse galloped home. The prince did not come home.

Everyone was seeking, seeking. The prince cannot be found. The court is in mourning, the emperor is weeping. Days and days go by. Then the next eldest prince said, 'I too will go hunting. I will go the way my brother went, and maybe I shall get news of him.'

So off he set; and he had but just ridden through the city gates when the hare sprang out from a bush. Off went the hare, off went the prince after it, this way, that way, over hill, over dale, till they came to the watermill. In through the open door of the mill darts the hare; out of the door comes the dragoness. She seizes the prince; the horse gallops home riderless. The prince is not seen again.

So then the emperor's youngest son said, 'I too will go hunting. I will take the road my brothers took, and maybe I shall get news of them.'

The emperor said, 'You shall not go! You shall stay with me. Must I lose you also?'

'Father, let me go!'

'No!'

'Father, let me go!'

'No! *No!*'

The prince said, 'I must and will go!'

And off he rode, and the emperor took to his bed for sorrowing.

Well, the prince had but just got through the city gates, when the hare jumped out of a bush. Off goes the hare, the prince after it, over hill, over dale, this way, and that way, till they come to the watermill. The hare darts in through the open door of the mill, but the prince does not think to go after it. He rode on in search of his brothers. Said he to himself, 'When I come back I shall find that hare.'

He rode a long way, over hill, over dale, through forest, through swamp, but he got no news of his brothers. So in the evening he went back to the mill. And at the door of the mill sat an old woman.

'God bless you, old mother!'

'God bless you, little son!'

'Old mother, have you seen a little hare?'

'Oh, my little son, that was no hare, that was a dragoness. Wherever she goes she destroys everything.'

Said the prince, 'Even my brothers?'

Said the old woman, 'Even your brothers, little son. Go home now whilst you are safe and sound, and not as they are.'

Said the prince, 'And you – why do you stay here?'

'Ah, my little son, I am her slave. I cannot help but stay.'

The prince said, 'Then I too will stay, and kill her.'

The old woman said, 'No one can do that, until they find her strength; and where that strength is, no one knows.'

The prince said, 'Try to find out where her strength is.'

The old woman said, 'I will try, little son. Go home now. Come again in the morning; and if I have news for you – well.'

So the prince rode home. And when the dragoness came back to the mill, the old woman fawned on her. 'Where has my dragoness been?' she said. 'Why won't my dragoness tell an old woman?'

The dragoness grinned with her great mouth, showing all her teeth. 'Old woman, I go a long, long way. I go where my strength is.'

'But why won't my dragoness tell her old woman why she goes so far? Why won't my dragoness say where her strength is? If this old woman knew, this old woman would run and kiss the place all over!'

'Well, old woman, my strength is in the stove yonder.'

The old woman ran and flung her arms round the stove. She kissed it all over.

The dragoness laughed like a wolf yelping. 'Silly old woman, my strength isn't there!'

'Then where is it?'

'In yonder tree trunk.'

The old woman ran and embraced the tree trunk. 'Happy, happy tree where my dragoness keeps her strength!' And she kissed the tree many times.

The dragoness rolled on the floor with laughing. 'Silly old noodle, my strength isn't there!'

'Then where is it?'

'I shan't tell you.'

'Not tell your old woman that loves you and serves you hand and foot? Oh, what a hard-hearted dragoness!'

'Much good it would do you if I should tell you!'

'Good! Why, I don't know what I should do for joy!'

So, after a bit more teasing, the dragoness said, 'Listen then. My strength lies where no one can reach it. In the next kingdom is a lake. In the lake is a dragon. In the dragon is a wild boar; in the wild boar is a dove; in the dove is a sparrow; and in the sparrow lies my strength . . . Now scratch my head, old woman, for I am drowsy and would sleep.'

So the old woman scratched the head of the dragoness, and the dragoness fell asleep. And in the morning the dragoness spread her wings and flew away.

The prince came back to the mill. 'Old mother, have you found out where lies the strength of the dragoness?'

'I have found out, little son.'

And she told him.

The prince goes home again, dresses himself in a shepherd's smock, takes a shepherd's crook in his hand, and sets off for the next kingdom. And when he gets to this next kingdom, he is asking everyone he meets if they know who has need of a shepherd.

Yes, they told him, the king needed one. So off with him to the king's palace. And no sooner had he come there than the serving men ran to the king crying out, 'A shepherd has come! A shepherd has come!'

The king said, 'Bring him to me.'

So they brought him to the king, and the king said, 'Lad, would you tend my flocks?'

'My king, I would.'

'But you must know the danger,' said the king. 'Do not let the sheep go near the lake that lies outside the city. The grass on the margin of that lake is green and sweet, and should you not prevent them the sheep will run to it. But take heed, lad, and as your life is precious to you, lead them somewhere else. For of all the sheep and of all the shepherds who go down to the margin of that lake not one has returned.'

The shepherd-prince answered, 'I will indeed be careful of the sheep, oh king!'

'Then go, lad, and my prayers go with you!'

The shepherd-prince bowed himself out of the king's presence and went to the market place. There he bought two greyhounds, a hawk, and a set of bagpipes. And next morning he drove the sheep to pasture. The king watched him go; the king's daughter watched him go. The shepherd-prince had an eye to the king's daughter, for she was very beautiful.

Driving the sheep before him, he passed out of the city. He had his hawk on his wrist, his bagpipes under his arm, and his two greyhounds running behind him. As soon as they were out of the city the sheep saw the lake. What happened? They took to their heels and rushed helter-skelter to feed on the sweet green grass that grew on its margin. Did the prince try to stop them? Not he! He put his hawk to perch on the branch of a tree, laid his bagpipes on the grass, and bade his hounds lie quiet. Then he took off his shoes and breeches, waded out into the lake and shouted, 'Oh, dragon! Oh, dragon! If you are not a coward, come out and fight!'

And from the depths of the lake a voice answered, 'I am coming, princeling!'

So then the dragon came out of the lake. He was huge, he was hideous, he was terrible! The prince caught him about the body, and they wrestled till mid-day.

And then the sun beat hot.

Then the dragon said, 'Let me go, my prince, that I may plunge my burning, matted head into the lake, and I will toss you high as heaven!'

But the prince said, 'Oh dragon, there is to me a royal maiden. If she would but come and kiss me on the brow, I would toss you higher yet!'

Then suddenly the dragon loosed his hold, and sank back into the lake.

The prince came out of the water; he tidied himself and sat him down to play on his pipes. The sheep nibbled the sweet green grass; and when the evening was come, the prince rounded them up, took his hawk from the tree, whistled to his greyhounds, and drove the sheep into the city, playing on his bagpipes as he went.

When he entered the city all the people ran out into the streets shouting, 'A miracle! A miracle!' for never before had any sheep or any shepherd returned from the lake. And the king sent for his shepherd.

'Lad, ask a boon, that I may reward you!'

But the shepherd-prince answered, 'We will speak of that at another time.'

The next morning the prince rose early, and drove the sheep straight to the lake. But the king sent two horsemen after him to watch what he did; and the horsemen rode to the top of a wooded hill, where they could see without being seen.

All happened as the day before. The prince set his hawk on the tree branch, laid his bagpipes on the grass, bade his hounds lie quiet, took off shoes and breeches and waded into the lake.

'Oh, dragon! Oh, dragon! If you are not a coward, come out and fight!'

'I am coming, princeling!'

Then out from the lake came the dragon, huge, hideous, terrible. The prince caught him about the body and they wrestled. And when the mid-day sun beat hot, the dragon said, 'Princeling, let me go, that I may plunge my burning, matted head under the water, and I will fling you to the height of heaven!'

But the prince answered, 'Dragon, you are talking nonsense. There is to me a royal maiden, and when she kisses me on the forehead, I shall toss you higher than heaven!'

So then the dragon loosed his hold and went back into the lake.

And in the evening the shepherd-prince drove the sheep home. He was playing on his bagpipes, his hawk was on his wrist, and his hounds were at heel.

When he entered the city the people crowded about him, shouting and cheering. And the two horsemen whom the king had sent to watch, went to the king and told him all.

The king sends for the princess. 'Daughter,' says he, 'tomorrow you must go to the lake with the shepherd.'

But she begins to weep and tremble. 'Oh, Papa, I am your only child, and will you send me to destruction?'

But the king said, 'Daughter, have courage. Have I not had many shepherds, and have not all of those who went to the lake perished? But this lad has been twice to the lake, and has wrestled with the dragon and returned uninjured. If you play your part, I think he will overcome this dragon.'

71

'I will play my part,' said the princess. 'But, oh, my father, I am sorely frightened!'

So on the morrow, when the prince drives the flock to the lake the princess goes with him. The shepherd-prince is cheery, cheerier than ever, but the princess is trembling and trying to hide her tears.

So the prince comforts her. 'All will be well,' says he, 'if you do what I ask of you. When the right moment comes, run up to me and kiss me. You have nothing to fear.'

They come to the lake. The sheep run to feed on the sweet green grass. The prince puts his hawk on the branch, his bagpipes on the ground, and bids his hounds lie quiet. He takes off his shoes and breeches, wades into the lake.

'Oh, dragon! Oh, dragon! If you are not a coward, come out and fight!'

The dragon comes. Huge he is! Terrible he is! Hideous he is! The prince grapples with him, and they fight until the scorching heat of noon.

Then the dragon said, 'Princeling, let me go, that I may cool my burning, matted head under the water. After that I will fling you to the heights of heaven!'

And the prince answered, 'Dragon, oh, dragon, there is to me a royal maiden, and when she kisses me upon the forehead I shall toss you higher yet.'

So then the princess ran forward and kissed the prince on the forehead, and on the eyes, and on each cheek; and the prince swung the dragon round three times and tossed him beyond the heights of heaven. And when the dragon fell to earth again he was smashed into little pieces. And as he fell to pieces a wild boar leaped out of him and ran. And the prince called to his greyhounds, 'After that boar! After him!' And the greyhounds pounced upon the boar and killed him. But out of the boar flies a pigeon; so the prince calls to his hawk, 'After that bird! After him!' And the hawk pounces on the pigeon and kills it. Then out of the pigeon flies a sparrow, and the

73

prince calls to his hawk, 'Catch that bird, my hawk, catch it and
bring it to me!'

So the hawk caught the sparrow, and brought it in her talons to
the prince. The prince held the sparrow in his hand and said, 'Now
tell me where my brothers are!'

'Do not, do not hurt me!' cried the sparrow. 'I will tell you
truly. In your father's kingdom is a watermill, and beside that
watermill grow three willow saplings. Cut down those three saplings and smite upon their roots. Then there will open before you
the iron grating of a huge cellar. In that cellar you will find as
many people, young and old, men, women and children, as would fill
a kingdom. And amongst them are your brothers. Now let me go!'

But the prince said, 'How can I let you go? You are the strength
of the dragoness.'

He had no mercy on that sparrow. He killed it then and there.
And there came from far away a long howl. And that howl was all
that was left of the dragoness.

By this time it was twilight. The prince tidied himself, rounded
up the sheep, took his hawk on his wrist, whistled to his greyhounds,
and drove the sheep back towards the city, playing on his bagpipes
as he went. His greyhounds ran at his heels, and beside him walked
the princess, still trembling with fright.

What a welcome in the city! Bands playing, people cheering,
children strewing flowers, the king coming out of his palace to
meet and embrace him. What reward was good enough for the
dragon-slayer? Would he accept the princess as his wife? 'Will you
have him, my girl, will you have him?'

The princess said, 'If I am reward enough, I will gladly have him.'

The prince said, 'You are all the reward I can ask or think.'

And he told them who he was – the son of the emperor.

So the prince and princess were married, and after that they set
out for the emperor's kingdom. When they came to the watermill,
the prince halted his escort, found the three willow saplings, cut
them down, and struck their roots. Instantly an iron grating opened

nder the roots, and from the cellar beneath a multitude of people treamed forth. The prince watched them coming out; he showered old among them, and bade them go each to his home. He was vatching, watching for his brothers. And the brothers came, last of ll.

They laughed, they wept, they embraced, they kissed. They set ut for the emperor's palace – the prince, the princess, the two rothers. And the emperor received them with joy that had no nding.

And the old woman, the slave of the dead dragoness? No, she vasn't forgotten. They brought her to the palace; they fed, lothed, and protected her. They made her the happiest old woman n all the world.

8 · The She-Bear

There was once a pretty little princess called Luciella. And early one morning the king, her father, sent for her and said, 'Luciella, dress yourself in your best robes and put jewels in your hair, for today King Pippo is coming to ask your hand in marriage.'

'But Papa, Papa,' cried Luciella, 'King Pippo is old and ugly, and I've heard that he has a very bad temper. I don't want to marry him!'

'You will do as you're told,' said her father. 'King Pippo is the richest monarch in all the world. I have but a little kingdom, King Pippo has a big one. If you don't marry him, King Pippo will make war on me and take my little kingdom from me. So go along, and make yourself ready to receive him.'

Princess Luciella ran out into the garden. She sat down under a rose bush and cried. 'I won't marry the ugly old thing,' she sobbed, 'I won't, I *won't*!'

And out from behind the rose bush stepped a tiny old man with a long white beard.

Said he, 'Little princess, pretty little princess, why are you crying?'

'Oh! Oh! Oh! My father says I must marry ugly old King Pippo, and I don't want to!'

'Well, if you don't want to marry him, you needn't,' said the tiny man. And he gave Luciella a little stick. 'Put this stick in your mouth,' said he, 'and it will turn you into a bear. I don't think King Pippo will want to marry a she-bear!'

'No, I'm sure he won't!' laughed Luciella. And she took the

ttle stick, gave the tiny man a kiss, and ran back into the palace.

That very morning ugly old King Pippo arrived. He scowled
ound at everybody and said, 'Where's my bride?'

'Her maidens are just now robing her,' said Luciella's father.
She will be down immediately.'

'Then tell her to hurry herself,' said King Pippo rudely.

So a page was sent scurrying upstairs to the princess's room,
where her maidens, having dressed her in a white robe trimmed
with pearls, had just finished combing out her long golden hair,
and were now setting a little crown of diamonds on her head.

Princess Luciella peeped at herself in the mirror and laughed.
Do I look pretty?' she asked.

'You look most beautiful,' said the maidens.

The princess laughed again.

'And will King Pippo be pleased with me?'

'Indeed he cannot fail to be pleased,' said the maidens. But they
thought, 'Oh what a shame to give our darling princess to that
ugly old wretch! And she laughs! How can she laugh?'

'Now bring me downstairs,' said Luciella.

The maidens brought the laughing Luciella downstairs. The
doors of the great hall were flung open. Musicians played softly.
'Her Royal Highness the princess Luciella!' cried the king's
herald.

But what should come ambling in but a huge, shaggy she-bear:
for princess Luciella had put the little stick in her mouth.

'Ah-ah-ah!' The ladies screamed and ran. The lords and the
pages jumped out of the windows. The princess's father dived
under the table. *Gr-gr-gr!* The bear ran about the hall, growling and
snarling. King Pippo drew his sword. The bear stood on her hind
legs and landed him a box on the ear that sent him sprawling. Then
she gave a roar that set all the gold and silver dishes tinkling, and
ran out of the palace.

'You will live to repent of this insult!' shouted King Pippo to
the princess's father. And he went home in a rage.

77

Meanwhile Luciella Bear was running, running. She ran till she came to a great forest. And in that forest she lived happily, feeding on honey and wild berries. The little stick in her mouth didn't worry her; it was so small that she could hold it easily in her cheek.

But one day she heard the sounds of hurrying footsteps. Who was coming? An enemy? Perhaps King Pippo himself! Luciella Bear hid behind a tree and watched. No, it wasn't King Pippo. It was a young prince who had lost his way and was wandering here and there in the hope of finding a path to lead him home.

But he didn't find a path to lead him home. All he found was a great shaggy she-bear, who leaped from behind the tree and came bounding towards him.

The prince was frightened: the bear was so very huge, and he was unarmed, except for a little dagger at his belt. But he drew that little dagger, and stood his ground manfully.

'If I am to die, I will at least die fighting!' he thought.

But what was this? The bear lay down at his feet, rolled over on her side, and wagged her stump of a tail. For the prince was very handsome, and Luciella Bear hadn't seen a human being for a long, long time; and glad indeed she was to see one now, and that one so much to her liking.

So, as she went on wagging her tail, and looking up at the prince with admiring eyes, he lost all fear of her. He stooped and patted her head. He took some cake from his wallet and held it out to her. And what did Luciella Bear do then? She sat up and begged.

The prince laughed. 'Well, my bear, I see that someone has taught you good manners. I think you haven't always lived in the wild. I think you must have been somebody's pet. So, what do you say – will you be my pet now, and come home with me?'

And Luciella Bear nodded her head, and said '*Hou-oom, gr-oum,*' which was the nearest she could get to 'yes'.

'Only, my bear,' said the prince, 'the trouble is I'm lost. I don't know the way out of this forest.'

Oh, but Luciella Bear knew the way, and this she tried to tell him with so many gruntings and noddings of her head and waving of her paws, that when she began walking away the prince followed her; and she soon brought him the quickest way out of the forest and back into his own kingdom.

And there they are now, walking side by side, the prince with his hand on Luciella Bear's head. And so he brought her to his palace.

The young prince was delighted with his new pet. He had a pretty little house built for her in the palace garden, by a fountain just under the window of his bedroom, so that he could look out and call to her first thing in the morning and last thing at night. He fed her with his own hands, and ordered everyone to treat her with the greatest respect. And she went in and out of her little house, just as she pleased, and drank from the fountain, and wandered about the garden at her will, and was so very gentle and charming in her ways that all the prince's servants came to love her.

Now by and by it came summertime and very hot, and Luciella

Bear panted with the heat inside her thick coat. So early one morning, before anyone was up, she took the stick out of her mouth and turned into a girl again. And the girl went to the fountain and bathed her hands and face. Then she sat down on the edge of the fountain, took a comb from her pocket and began combing out her long golden hair. And the rising sun shone on that golden hair and made a glory of it. And whilst she combed her hair, princess Luciella was singing to herself, very very softly, for she was thinking that no one could see or hear her.

But someone did see and hear her, and that was the prince. For he too had felt stifled by the heat, and he had risen from his bed. There he was now, standing at his open window, looking down into the garden.

And what does the prince see down there, down there in the garden? He sees a maiden more beautiful than he had ever imagined a maiden could be. 'Oh! Oh!' He turns from the window, runs downstairs, and out at the great palace door.

But in his hurry he didn't think to open that door quietly, and the clatter he made startled Luciella, and quicker than quick she snatched up the stick and put it back into her mouth; so that all the prince saw when he ran to the fountain was his great shaggy bear ambling to meet him with love in her eyes.

'No, no, dear bear, it's not you I want!' cried the prince. 'The maiden, the maiden, where has she gone? Oh, my bear, you must have seen her! As you love me, lead me to her, my bear, and I'll give you a golden collar with diamond studs!'

But Luciella Bear turned her back on him and went into her little house, and the prince ran about the garden, searching, searching. Of course he didn't find the maiden, though he had all his servants searching for her till nightfall. So what happened? He took to his bed and fell into a fever, and not a doctor in the kingdom could cure him.

In his fevered dreams it seemed to the prince that he was out in the garden again, running after a maiden, and that he was just about to catch her when she laughed and turned into a bear. And, he woke, flinging out his arms and crying, 'Oh, my bear, my bear, my cruel, cruel bear!'

Now it so happened that the queen, his mother, was standing by his bed when he called out. And she said to herself, 'Then it is the bear who has caused my son's sickness! The creature must be a witch who has cast an evil spell on him!'

Then the queen hurried out of the prince's room, summoned a groom to her and said, 'Take a sword and kill that bear at once!'

But the groom isn't going to kill the bear, not he! He's much too fond of her. So what does he do? He coaxes her away into the forest with sweet cakes, ties her to a tree and lays a pile of food at her feet. 'I will come every day and feed you,' says he, and so leaves her.

The queen was watching by the prince's bed. 'As soon as the bear is dead, his sickness will leave him,' she thought. 'Oh, my son, my dear son, in a few moments now you will be yourself again!'

And she sent a page to bring the groom up to her; and when he came she whispered, 'Have you killed the bear?'

The groom looks her straight in the eyes, and lies bravely. 'Yes, your majesty, I have killed the bear.'

The prince hears, he gives a shout, leaps from his bed, snatches up his sword and runs at the groom. 'You murderer of all my hopes! Now you shall die, and when I have killed you, I will kill myself!'

The queen screams, the groom cries out in panic, 'No, no, my prince, I lied, I lied! I haven't killed your bear – how could I do such a cruel thing? I have only taken her into the forest and left her there, tied to a tree.'

Sick as he was, the prince huddled on some clothes, staggered from the room and down to the stables, scrambled on to his horse, more dead than alive, and galloped off to the forest. There he found his bear, and sobbing with pity and relief, he cut the rope that bound her, and brought her back to the palace.

She was glad enough to follow him.

By the time the prince had got back into the garden, he was raving again, and he cried to her, 'My bear, my bear, take off your skin, take off your skin! If you love me at all, if you wish me to live and not to die, *take off your skin!*'

But Luciella Bear walked away into her little house.

So then the prince flung himself back to bed, turned his face to the wall, and wept. And the queen, his mother, came and sat by the bed. 'My dear son, what causes this heartbreaking grief? Tell me, only tell me, that I may help and comfort you!'

And the prince answered, 'Nothing can comfort me but my bear. If you want me to live, have her brought to my room. I want no one else to look after me, I want no one else to smooth my bed, I want no one else to cook my food, I want no one else to tidy my room, but only my bear.'

'This is madness!' thought the queen. But she had the bear brought to his room. And the bear came over to the bed. She took the prince's hand between her great paws.

And the prince smiled. 'My bear,' said he, 'it is a long time since I tasted food. But if *you* would cook me something, I believe I would eat it. Won't you cook me something, my darling bear?'

'*Hou-oum, gr-oum,*' said Luciella Bear, nodding her head.

'Mother,' said the prince, 'send for a cooking stove and a pan, and a chicken and herbs and seasoning.'

'Oh, my poor son, he is quite, quite crazy!' thinks the queen. But she did what he asked her.

So there was the stove, and the bear lit it. There was the pan, and the bear put it on the stove. There was the chicken, and the bear put it in the pan with the herbs and the seasoning. And when the chicken was cooked, the bear laid it neatly in a dish, and brought it to the prince. And the prince, who for days had not been able to swallow down so much as a spoonful of soup, ate up everything, scraped the dish, and licked his fingers.

'That was the most delicious food I have ever tasted!' said he.

So, when he had finished eating, the bear handed him a glass of wine, and she did it with so much grace that the queen felt ready to kiss her. As for the prince, he jumped out of bed and put on his clothes; and the bear re-made the bed, and tidied up the room; and then she went into the garden, and came back with great armfuls of roses; these she strewed all over the bed. And the queen thought, 'This bear is indeed a treasure! No wonder my son loves her!'

But the prince has remembered his dreams again. He turns pale as death. 'Oh, my lady mother,' he cries, 'if my bear will not kiss me, I believe my spirit will leave my body!'

And the queen, fearing to see her son fall into a mad fit again, said to the bear, 'My dear creature, kiss him, kiss him quickly!'

Luciella Bear goes to the prince; she lays her muzzle against his face. The prince seizes her by both cheeks. What happens? The stick falls out of the bear's mouth – and there is the prince holding in his arms the most beautiful princess that ever the sun shone on.

'Oh, my love, my love, my love, I have found you at last!'

'Yes,' laughed princess Luciella, 'you have found me!' And she told him all her sad little story. And just as the story had come to an end, who should jump out from among the heap of roses on the bed, but the tiny old man with the long white beard.

'Princess, pretty little princess,' says he, 'once I saw you crying, now I see you laughing. You won't want my stick any more, so I'll take it back again.' And take it back he did. 'All stories should have happy endings,' says he, as he hops through the window. 'And what happier ending can there be than that a lovely princess should marry a handsome prince?'

The lovely princess did marry the handsome prince. The king, the princess's father, came to the wedding. Poor man, he had been living in fear all this time, lest King Pippo should send an army and take his little kingdom from him. But the prince said, 'I have a bigger army even than King Pippo, and I am on your side. Let King Pippo come if he dare!'

King Pippo didn't dare. So the prince, the princess and the princess's father lived in peace and happiness all their lives.

9 · The Frog

There was a king who had three sons, straight, tall and handsome, with eyes like bright falcons. And one day the king said, 'My bright falcons, it is time you were married. Take your silver bows and your copper arrows, go into the courtyard and each of you shoot one shot. Where the arrows fall, there you will find your brides.'

The three princes went out into the courtyard and each shot an arrow. The arrow of the eldest flew, flew, it flew right into another kingdom, where a princess was walking in the palace garden. The arrow fell at the princess's feet; she picked it up and took it to the king, her father.

'Look, Papa, I have found a copper arrow! What shall I do with it?'

Her father said, 'Keep it. Give it to none until the one comes who claims you as his bride.'

The eldest prince had set out on horseback to follow his arrow. He came into the other kingdom, met the princess walking in the palace garden and said, 'I have come for my arrow.'

The princess said, 'No one shall have it but the one who takes me for his bride.'

The prince said, 'I will take you for my bride.'

So then and there they were betrothed. And the eldest prince rode home again.

Meanwhile the second prince had shot his arrow. It flew, flew, and fell in the courtyard of a duke's castle. The duke's daughter was sitting on the steps before the door. The arrow fell at her feet; she picked it up and took it to the duke, her father.

'Look, Papa, I have found a copper arrow! What shall I do with it?'

The duke said, 'Keep it. Give it to none until the one comes who claims you as his bride.'

The second prince had set out to follow his arrow. He came into the courtyard of the duke's castle. The duke's daughter was sitting on the steps outside the door.

The prince said, 'I have come for my arrow.'

The duke's daughter said, 'No one shall have it but the one who takes me for his bride.'

The second prince said, 'I will take you for my bride.'

So they were betrothed, and the second prince rode home again.

Meanwhile the youngest prince, whose name was Ivan, had shot his arrow. It flew, flew and landed in a swamp. Ivan went to the swamp after his arrow. On a mound in the middle of the swamp sat a green frog clasping the arrow in her arms.

Said Ivan, 'I have come for my arrow.'

Said the frog, 'I give it only to the one who takes me for his bride.'

Ivan went home, very troubled.

Then the king called the three princes before him and said, 'Tell me, my bright falcons, of the brides you have found.'

The eldest prince said, 'I have found a king's daughter.'

The second prince said, 'I have found a duke's daughter.'

Ivan wept, and said nothing.

The king said, 'Ivan, why do you weep?'

Ivan said, 'How should I not weep? My brothers have found their brides, but I have found only a green frog in a swamp. Is this fitting?'

The king said, 'Take her, my son, she is your fate.'

So the eldest prince rejoiced and married the princess. The second prince rejoiced and married the duke's daughter. But Ivan was married to the green frog; and if the frog rejoiced, Ivan did not.

The king gave each of his sons a beautiful little house to live in with their wives. And one day he said, 'Now I will see which of my daughters-in-law is most skilled in weaving. Let each of them weave me a piece of cloth, and let them bring the cloths to me tomorrow morning.'

That night Ivan wept. The frog said, 'Ivan, my husband, why do you weep?'

'How should I not weep? The king my father bids each of his daughters-in-law to weave him a cloth. How should *you* weave a cloth?'

The frog said, 'Don't weep. Go to bed and sleep. The morning is wiser than the evening.'

Ivan goes to bed and sleeps. What does his wife do? She takes off her frog skin. Look! There she stands now a beautiful maiden, none more beautiful. She goes down into the courtyard, she calls, she whistles – there stands a loom. She snaps her white fingers – and skeins of coloured silk fall to her right hand and her left hand. She gathers up the skeins of silk, stands at the loom and weaves

86

those silks into the finest of cloths, emblazoned with eagles. She goes back into the house, lays the cloth beside Ivan's pillow, and puts on her frog skin again.

In the morning Ivan woke. There was the fine cloth, none finer in the world. He took it joyfully to the king, and the king said, 'This is indeed beautiful! Never have I seen anything more beautiful! It shall hang on the back of my throne. But as for the work of my other two daughters-in-law – Bah! It isn't fit to be seen. Throw it on the ash heap! And now let me see which of the three can bake me the best cakes.'

And Ivan went home weeping.

The frog said, 'Ivan, my husband, why do you weep?'

Ivan said, 'How should I not weep? The king my father has bidden you bake him some cakes. How can a frog bake cakes?'

The frog said, 'Don't weep. Go to bed and sleep. The morning is wiser than the evening.'

So Ivan went to bed and slept.

Then the eldest son's wife said to the second son's wife, 'What shall I do? I have never baked a cake in my life!'

'Neither have I,' said the second son's wife. 'Let us watch the frog and see what she does. Then we will do the same.'

And they went to Ivan's house and looked in through the kitchen window.

The frog was on the table mixing batter. She was pouring more and more water into the batter till it was streaming wet. She took the batter, climbed on to the kitchen stove, and laid the batter on the hot slab. The batter bubbled and steamed and flowed all over the stove.

The other two wives ran to their houses and did the same. They had a fine burnt mess for their night's work.

But as soon as they are gone from the window – what does Ivan's wife do? She takes off her frog skin and becomes a beautiful maiden, none more beautiful. She calls, she whistles: there now on the table is a bowl full of creamy batter. She snaps her white fingers:

there now are delicious little cakes baking in the oven. And when the cakes are ready she takes them out of the oven, lays them on a silver tray beside Ivan's pillow. Then she puts on her frog skin again.

In the morning Ivan woke: there were the cakes. Oh, oh, never had he seen such cakes! Joyfully he ran with them to the king. Oh, oh, the king eats one, he eats another, he eats the lot.

'These are the most delicious cakes that ever I tasted!' says he. 'But as to those messes my other daughters-in-law have made – throw them to the dogs!'

So they threw them to the dogs; but the dogs wouldn't eat them.

The next thing the king did was to appoint a day for a great banquet, at which his three sons were to appear with their wives.

And when Ivan heard of it, he went home weeping.

Says the frog, 'Ivan, my husband, why do you weep?'

Says Ivan, 'How should I not weep? In three days' time the king my father is to give a banquet to which we three sons must bring our wives. How can I take *you* to a banquet, my frog? I shall be mocked by all the courtiers and all the guests!'

The frog said, 'Sleep now, Ivan my husband, all will be well.'

So the day of the banquet came, and Ivan was sad as sad. But the frog said, 'Go on ahead, my husband. When the rain begins to fall, know that your wife washes herself in raindrops. When lightning flashes, know that your wife is arraying herself. When thunder rolls, know that your wife is coming.'

So Ivan puts on his finest clothes, mounts his horse, and rides off to his father's palace.

The brothers and their wives had already arrived. The brothers were richly clad; the wives were dressed in silk embroidered with gold and silver, and wore diamond necklaces.

And the brothers mock Ivan. 'What, Ivan, you have come alone? Where is your wife? Couldn't you have brought her tied up in a handkerchief?'

'She will come soon,' says Ivan.

Then rain began to patter on the palace roof, and Ivan said, 'Now my dear wife washes herself in the raindrops.'

And the brothers mocked, 'Ivan, are you crazy?'

Then lightning flashed and Ivan said, 'Now my dear wife is arraying herself for the banquet.'

And the brothers looked at one another and shrugged. 'Yes, he is mad!' they whispered.

Then came such a clap of thunder that the whole palace shook. 'Now comes my wife, my little dove!' said Ivan.

The words were scarcely out of his mouth before a glass coach drawn by eight fiery horses dashed into the palace yard. And out of the coach and up into the banqueting hall stepped a princess, so beautiful, so beautiful that everyone held their breath.

'She is so beautiful, so beautiful, it is not to be told!' whispers the king to the queen.

'Yes, so beautiful, so beautiful, her like is not on earth!' whispers the queen to the king.

Then the king rose, led the beautiful princess to the table and set her on his right hand. And everyone began to eat.

The frog princess had a strange way with her. With everything she ate she put a little bit in her mouth, and a little bit in her right sleeve. And with everything she drank, she put a little drop in her mouth, and a little drop in her left sleeve. And the other brothers' wives watched and copied her: a bit in the mouth, a bit in the right sleeve; a drop in the mouth, a drop in the left sleeve. It didn't seem to them a pleasant way of eating and drinking; but they weren't going to be outdone by a frog, even if she had turned into a princess more beautiful than the sun.

When the feast is over, they all troop out into the courtyard. Music plays. Now they are going to dance.

The king said, 'Let my sons and their wives lead out the dance.'

But the wives of the two elder brothers said, 'Let Ivan and his wife dance first.' For they thought, 'Even if she is lovely she was

born in a swamp – and how should she learn to dance? Oh ho
now she will be put to shame!'

So Ivan and his wife led out the dance. And the frog princess
moved so lightly, so beautifully, that her feet scarcely touched the
floor, and everyone watched in amazement. Surely never since the
world began had there been such dancing!

And by and by the frog princess bade Ivan sit down, for she had
a mind to dance by herself. Off she goes, then, skimming over the
floor like a swallow over a pond. She waves her right sleeve: a
little bit falls out of it. And the little bit turns into a garden. In
the middle of the garden stands a pillar, and on the pillar is a
white cat running up, running down. When the cat runs up he
sings songs. When he runs down he tells stories.

Off goes the princess again, skimming over the ground like any
swallow. She waves her left sleeve: a little drop falls out of it.
There now flowing through the garden is a little river with white
swans swimming on it. The company watch breathless. But
when the princess sits down to rest, the courtyard echoes with
cheers.

'Now let my two other daughters-in-law see what *they* can do!'
cried the king.

So the elder brother's wife, and the second brother's wife got
up to dance, though they didn't much want to. They danced,
danced, whirled, twirled; they were doing their best, poor things,
but the king was frowning. So one daughter-in-law waved her
right sleeve, and a bone flew out of it and hit the king on the forehead; the other daughter-in-law waved her left sleeve. *Splash!* A
deluge of wine and soup flew into the king's eye.

'Enough, enough!' cried the king. 'You clumsy fools! Sit down
before you blind me! Take your partners, gentlemen, and let the
dance become general.'

So the guests danced and the courtiers danced, and the frog
princess sat and watched. But Ivan ran to the stable, jumped on
his horse and galloped back to his own little house. Could that

onderful princess really be his wife, or would he find his frog at
ome?

Up into the frog's room he ran. What did he see? A frog skin
·ing on the floor. 'Oh my dove, my wife, my beautiful one!' he
ried. 'Never, never shall you turn into a frog again!' And he picked
p the frog skin and thrust it into the fire. Then he rode back to
1e palace.

At dawn the party broke up and Ivan went home with his wife.
he went into her room and looked about. Said she, 'Where is my
arment?'

Said Ivan, 'If you mean your frog skin, I have burned it.'

Said she, 'Alas! Alas! Ivan, my Ivan, what have you done?
Without my skin I am forbidden to remain here. Seek for me on
he mountain of glass, if so be that you may ever win there!
Goodbye, goodbye, my Ivan!'

And she waves her hand, turns into a cuckoo, and flies out of
he window.

Ivan wasted no moment. He ran to the stable, leaped on his
10rse and galloped off. Where was he going? He didn't know. But
ind his princess again he must and would.

He rode, rode, rode, asking all he met if they could tell him of
he mountain of glass; but no one could. Until, one day, tired out
ind nigh despairing, he met with a little old man, white as milk.

'Whither away, my friend?' said the little old man.

'To seek my wife on the mountain of glass. Do you know, little
old one, where it may be?'

'How should I not know? Certainly I know!'

'Then tell me, tell me!'

'Why should I tell you, my son? It is the same whether I tell
you or not, for I think you will never win there. It would take the
bravest man in the world to reach that mountain. Go home, my
son, and live in safety.'

Ivan drew his sword. 'Will you tell me, little old one, or shall I
cut off your head?'

The little old man laughed. 'I see you have a stout heart.' And
he took a ball out of his pocket. 'Roll this ball before you – go
where it leads. It will show you the way to the glass mountain that
stands at the end of the world.'

Ivan thanks the old man, takes the ball, and throws it before him.
Off rolls the ball, and after it gallops Ivan. Over hill, over dale,
through forest, bog, and fen he rode, rode till he came to the end
of the world. And there, towering up into the sky before him, rose
the glass mountain. Round the mountain flowed a great river; over
the river stretched a narrow bridge; and beyond the bridge stood
three giants keeping guard. And the ball stops rolling. It will not
cross the bridge.

Ivan was about to gallop over the bridge, ball or no ball, when
there, barring his way, stood the little old man, white as milk.

'Stop, stop! Don't you see the giants?'

'Yes, I see them. What of it?'

'There is this of it,' said the little old man; 'if you cross the
bridge now, they will tear you limb from limb, and eat you mouthful by mouthful. Will that save your princess?'

'But save her I must and will!'

'Then wait, wait, Impatience!' said the little old man. 'At sunset
the giants lie down to sleep. Then you may cross. But take these
four cloths and wrap them about your horse's hoofs, lest by his
clattering on the bridge he wake the giants. Nevertheless, as soon
as you have passed them, the giants will wake, and start after you.
Here is a packet of dust. When you have passed the giants and they
wake, throw the dust behind you. The dust will fill the giants'
eyes, and they will see nothing. And so you will escape. Beyond
the river you will find a mill. Ask the miller for a night's lodging.
At supper the cook will bring him a roast cock. He will eat it all
himself, refusing you a mouthful. The bones of the cock he will
order his cook to throw under the mill wheel. But give her a piece
of gold that she may hide them for you. And when the miller
sleeps, be off with you to the glass mountain, taking the bones

with you. Throw them at the mountain, one after the other; they will make steps for you to climb by. At the top of the mountain you will meet the witch, the Bony-Legged. Remember your manners, Ivan, and don't vex her: she holds your wife's life in her hands . . . And so farewell to you. In this world we shall not meet again.'

Ivan had scarcely time to thank the old man, before that old man vanished.

Ivan bound the four cloths round the four hoofs of his horse, and waited till sunset. Then the giants lay down and slept. Ivan crossed the bridge; his horse's hoofs made no sound. Nevertheless the giants started up the moment he had passed them. So he shook the dust out of the packet; and then, though it was still day before him, it was night behind him. And the giants stumbled here and there in the night, seeking but not finding.

Ivan rides on and comes to a mill.

Says the miller, 'What do you want?'

Says Ivan, 'A night's lodging.'

Says the miller, 'I give no common man lodging.'

Says Ivan, 'But I am a prince, and can pay you handsomely.'

So then the miller lets him come in, and they sit down to supper.

The miller ate and ate, and towards the end of the meal, the cook brought in a roasted cock.

'You eat none of this,' said the miller to Ivan. 'This is *my* dish!'

And he gobbled up the whole cock, and bade the cook throw the bones behind the mill wheel.

But Ivan had already given the cook a piece of gold, and she hid the bones under her apron; and when the miller had gone to bed and was soundly snoring, she brought the bones to Ivan.

'And what good they may do you is none of my business,' said she.

So Ivan took the bones and rode off to the foot of the glass mountain. He threw one bone at the mountain: there was a step. He got on to that step and threw another bone. Another step. And so on with him, up and up, throwing the bones before him, and

the bones making steps, till at sunrise he reached the top of th
mountain.

What did he see? A great glass castle. And at the door of th
castle stood the old witch, Bony-Legged.

'Ah, the handsome young man!' cries old Bony-Legged. 'Com
in, come in, my precious! Tell me, None-So-Handsome, what d
you want of me?'

Ivan bows low. 'I have come for my princess, my dear wife.'

'Well, well, I will give her to you, but first you must do me
little service.'

'I will gladly serve you, madam,' says Ivan.

Old Bony-Legged took him to a garden behind the castle; and in
the garden was a big pond. 'I have been waiting for years to have
this pond bailed dry,' says old Bony-Legged. 'Empty it for me and
you shall have your princess. Here is your bailer.'

Then she gave Ivan a thimble with a hole in it. 'If the pond is
dry by sunset, well and good. If not, I shall have to cook you for
my supper, None-So-Handsome.'

And so back with her into the castle, screeching with laughter.

Ivan throws the thimble into the pond, and begins to bail out
the water with his cupped hands. But the hours go by, and the
more water he bails out, the fuller the pond becomes. The sun is
going down the sky: it will soon set . . . He will never empty that
pond; he will never win back his princess; old Bony-Legged is
going to have him for her supper – no doubt about it!

Ivan flings himself down on the ground and weeps.

'Ivan, my husband, why do you weep?'

Ivan sprang to his feet. 'My love, my beautiful one, my princess!'

Yes, it was indeed his princess.

The princess waved her little white hand over the pond. And
behold, the pond was dry!

'Now we are saved!' cries Ivan. 'Come, let us go from here,
quickly, quickly!'

'Not yet,' says the princess. 'We have still to deal with the witch

who has held me in her power these many years. When she find
the pond dry, she will take the shape of a rain cloud, a huge dark
cloud. Draw your sword, Ivan, and when that cloud comes, a
come it will, look well at it and strike where the darkness i
thickest.'

And scarcely had the princess spoken, when, sure enough, a black
darkness of cloud came rushing from the castle. It was all black
but blackest near the ground, and there Ivan struck with his sword
The darkness screams, the darkness vanishes: and there on the
ground lies old Bony-Legged, pierced through the heart.

Then the princess turned herself into a cuckoo, took Ivan unde
her wing, and flew with him down from the mountain, and pas
the mill, and over the heads of the giants, and across the bridge
And there she set him down, turned back into her own beautifu
shape, and called and whistled.

And Ivan's horse, when he heard the whistle, came galloping
over the bridge. And Ivan and the princess got a-horseback and
rode to their home, where they lived happily, none more happily
for ever after.

10 · Princess Felicity

Once upon a time a prince went to the king, his father, and said, 'Father, I am now of age; it is time I took a wife.'

The king said, 'Well, my son, you shall take a wife.' And he showed the prince a book in which were pictured all the princesses in the world: fair princesses, dark princesses, lovely princesses, plain princesses – princesses without number.

'Choose which you will,' said the king to the prince.

The prince turned the leaves of the book, looked at the portrait of this princess, of that princess: no, none pleased him – until he turned to the very last page.

'Father, father!' cried he. '*This* is the princess who shall be my wife!'

The king said, 'My son, that is the princess Felicity, and she is indeed the beauty of the world. But she lives in an enchanted place; it is not possible for a man to come there. Many have tried, none has succeeded.'

The prince said, 'I must and will succeed!'

And he jumped on to his horse and set off to seek for the princess Felicity. He took with him a faithful servant; and he took with him a dainty little carriage drawn by eight small ponies, with a little coachman in green and gold holding the reins, and a little footman standing up behind. Why did he take the little carriage? Well, to be sure, it was to bring the princess back in.

So off they go: prince, faithful servant, carriage, coachman, footman and all. They journey all day, and when night falls they are in the middle of a big dark wood. No finding their way through

97

that big wood in the darkness, so there they have to stop. They unharness, feed and hobble the two horses and the eight ponies; they make a good supper from the food they have brought with them; and then the prince, and the little coachman, and the little footman lie down and sleep. But the faithful servant stays awake. He listens and watches.

At midnight he heard voices above his head: it was the winds talking in the trees.

'Brother, what news from France?' said the wind from Spain.

And the wind from France answered, 'The king's son has set out to seek the princess Felicity, but he will never reach her.'

'Is there no way to reach her?' says the wind from Spain.

'Yes, there is a way,' says the wind from France. 'But the prince does not know it. No one in the world knows it, except myself. The princess is shut up in a castle, twenty miles from here. I have blown round that castle many's the time, and set the black flag on its ramparts flapping. But the castle is guarded by fierce beasts who never sleep, except when the great castle bell tolls twelve noon. Then the fierce beasts fall to the ground and sleep for one hour. It is during that hour alone that one can reach the princess, and then only if one is not stopped by enchantments. For the castle is filled with beautiful maidens who seek to waylay with their charms any man who has managed to enter; and if that man so much as turns his head towards the maidens, he is lost forever. Nor is that all. The would-be deliverer must have on his finger the Ring of Virtue, which is hidden at the very top of a tall tree a hundred paces from the castle. For when the wild beasts wake and find the princess gone, they will set off in pursuit. And in front of those who flee will open a deep, fast-flowing river: a river none may cross save he who wears on his finger the Ring of Virtue.'

'Yes, I see that to rescue the princess is impossible,' said the wind from Spain. 'For who among mortal men can know these things you have told me? . . . And so goodnight, brother!'

The wind from Spain then flew to the north; the wind from
France flew to the south. And in the forest was a great silence.

And the faithful servant kept all that he had heard a secret in his
heart.

At dawn he woke his master, the prince, and the little coachman
and the little groom. They breakfasted, fed the horses and the
ponies, harnessed them, and went their way.

They soon came out of the forest and found themselves on a
pleasant road. And along that pleasant road they travel all day, and
in the evening come to the house of a good old man, whom the
prince greets courteously.

'And where might you be going, my prince, with your horses and
your little carriage?' asks the good old man.

'I am going to seek the princess Felicity.'

'Ah!' says the old man. 'I have watched ride by my house
thousands and thousands of princes and brave soldiers, all on their
way to deliver the princess Felicity. But up till now I have seen not
one return.'

The prince said, 'I shall return.'

'May be, may be,' said the old man. 'But you are weary. Come in,
rest and eat.'

It was pleasant in the old man's house, and the prince decided to
stay there for a day or two, to refresh both himself and his little
retinue. But in the morning the faithful servant said, 'Sire, have I
your permission to take a ride and explore the country?'

'By all means, if that is your wish,' said the prince.

The faithful servant rode off. Where was he going? He was
going to find the princess Felicity. He rode, rode, came over a hill,
and there in the valley below him he saw the castle he sought. He
knew it by the black flag that floated from the ramparts. So he rode
down into the valley; and in a meadow some three hundred paces
from the castle stood a tall solitary tree.

Thinks he, 'That must be the tree the wind spoke of, the tree
whose topmost branches hide the Ring of Virtue.' And he tied his

horse to the tree, climbed up, found the ring and put it on his finger. Then he came down and walked on towards the castle.

'The sun is right above my head,' thinks he. 'Surely it must be twelve noon.' And he opened the castle gates and stepped into a garden where many trees grew.

But it was not twelve noon; it was just a quarter to twelve. The fierce beasts were wide awake, they heard him, they smelt him, they came raging towards him. Now they would tear him to pieces. But he leaped up into a tree. The wild beasts, roaring terribly, flung themselves on the tree to uproot it. They tore at the ground with such fury that the faithful servant had only just time to leap into another tree before the first tree toppled. But at that moment the great castle bell tolled the first stroke of noon, and the beasts fell to the ground and lay as the dead.

Into the castle runs the faithful servant. He runs from room to room, from hall to hall, seeking the princess. And in every room, and in every hall, beautiful maidens came smiling to meet him, whispering in sweet soft voices, 'Ah, handsome young man, stop a little while with us!' But he ran past them, and though they called after him most plaintively, even to sobbing out, 'Young man, young man, what have we done that you should scorn us so?' he just ran on and never turned his head.

And at last he came to the room where Princess Felicity sat all alone, working at an embroidery frame.

Princess Felicity dropped her needle and jumped to her feet. 'Who are you?' she cried. 'And how have you come here, where no man comes?'

But he only answered, 'Hasten! Hasten!' caught her by the hand and ran with her out of the castle, through the garden, and out into the meadow; untied his horse from the tree, leaped into the saddle, snatched her up on to the crupper behind him, and off with him at full gallop.

Behind them the great bell of the castle tolled one. The fierce beasts roused and looked about them. The castle gates stood open, and out into the castle garden ran the beautiful maidens, crying, 'The princess Felicity is stolen, is stolen!'

With furious roarings the fierce beasts set off in pursuit. The faithful servant is galloping, galloping, but the fierce beasts are catching up on him; and before him now flows a river so wide, so deep, so fast rushing, that there is no getting through it.

'Ring of Virtue,' cries the faithful servant, 'may this river open itself and let me pass!'

Immediately the river dried up; the faithful servant galloped across its rocky bed; but the fierce beasts were close behind – roaring and howling they pounded down into the dry river bed. Ah, they will have him yet! But when those fierce beasts reached the middle of the river bed, the faithful servant cried out, 'Ring of Virtue, let the river flow again!'

And the river flowed again. It came rushing furiously with all its foaming waves, it whirled the fierce beasts here, it whirled them there, it carried them away in its foaming waves, it drowned them all. And the faithful servant brought the princess Felicity to his master.

Next morning the prince said goodbye to the good old man, and the little cavalcade set out on its homeward journey, the princess seated in the pony carriage, the joyful prince riding close at her side, the faithful servant following.

Night found them deep in the forest where they had slept on first setting out, so there they decided to sleep and wait for morning. The faithful servant cut down boughs and made three leafy arbours: one for the princess Felicity, one for the prince, one for himself and the little coachman and the little groom.

'Why go to all this trouble?' said the prince. 'The night is warm and we have our cloaks.'

'It is best to be protected from the night winds,' said the faithful servant.

And what did he do next? He took the horses and the little ponies and tethered them afar off.

'Why do you do that?' said the prince.

'Lest they should stamp and whinny and disturb the princess,' said the faithful servant.

'It seems you are full of whims tonight!' said the prince.

They ate the food the good old man had provided, and then they went into the leafy arbours and lay down. The princess slept, the prince slept, the coachman and the little groom slept. But the faithful servant lay awake, listening with all his ears.

At midnight he heard voices above his head. It was the winds talking in the trees.

'Someone was listening the other night,' said the wind from France. 'We must search lest someone is again hidden in the wood.' And they began searching leaf by leaf among the trees. They felt over the three arbours with their long fingers, but they felt only branches and leaves.

'There is no one here,' said the wind from Spain. 'What is there of news?'

'The princess Felicity has been freed,' said the wind from France. 'But the prince will not succeed in taking her home. On the way they will meet a grape seller, and the princess, who loves grapes, will wish to eat them. But if she touches them, she dies. And even if she escapes that danger, there is another awaiting her. You know that on their way home they come to a road that runs

along the banks of a little river. And in the river the princess will
see a man flinging up his arms and crying out that he is drowning.
The princess will run to help him, but if she but touches the hand of
that man, she will die.'

'Yes, I see that the princess is as good as dead,' said the wind
from Spain. 'For how should the prince know of these dangers to
prevent them? And so goodnight, brother.'

The wind from Spain then flew to the south; the wind from
France flew to the north. And in the forest was a great silence.

At dawn the faithful servant roused the rest of the party. They
breakfasted, harnessed the horses and the little ponies, and set off
once more on their homeward journey: princess Felicity seated in
her little carriage, the prince on horseback riding close to the
carriage, the faithful servant riding behind them.

'Today we shall reach home!' said the prince joyfully.

Towards noon they came to a fork in the road, and there stood a
man calling out, 'Beautiful grapes for sale! Beautiful grapes!'

'Oh, oh!' cried the princess. 'I love grapes, I will buy some!'

'No, no,' said the faithful servant, 'those grapes are not good.'

'They look good to me,' said the princess.

And she makes to get out of the carriage.

But the faithful servant leaps from his horse. 'My princess, if you
really desire the grapes, I will buy them for you.'

And he ran to the grape seller, and bought a basketful of grapes.

But unseen of anybody, he thrusts his fist into the basket,
crushes the grapes, and dips the basket into some stagnant water by
the roadside. Then he carries the basket to the princess.

'You see, princess, the grapes are rotten, and they smell bad.'

'Bah! Throw them away!' says the princess.

So the faithful servant threw away the basket of grapes.

They travelled on. Soon their road ran by the banks of a small
river, and they heard a voice crying, 'Help! Help! Help! I am
drowning!'

'Ah!' cried the princess. 'We must save that poor man!'

'No!' cried the faithful servant. 'Let him drown!'

But the princess jumped from the carriage and ran to the river.

'Help! Help!' cries the voice again; and a man's head and wildly threshing arm appears above the surface of the water. The princess reaches out to seize the arm; but before she can grasp it, the faithful servant has drawn his sword. *Slash!* There goes the arm floating down the river; and the man's head has disappeared under the water.

'Villain!' cried the prince. 'You have murdered a helpless man!' And he plunged his dagger into the faithful servant's heart.

The little company travelled on; but the faithful servant lay dead on the river bank; and his riderless horse galloped whinnying up and down by the water.

And the prince brought Princess Felicity safely home, and took her to wife.

What a wedding that was! Every conduit in the city ran with wine; braziers flamed at street corners, and over the braziers stood ovens filled with roasting pork and venison. The citizens ate, drank, danced, sang; and when night came the whole countryside was ablaze with fireworks.

The prince lived in rapture; but the princess Felicity was not quite happy. She was troubled by strange dreams, and one night she heard a voice saying, 'Wretch that you are! You have slain the one who delivered you. If you had eaten of those grapes, or if you had touched the hand of the drowning man, you would have instantly fallen dead.'

In the morning she told the prince what she had heard. And he, too, became troubled.

'If it is true,' said he, 'what a villain I am! But is it true? Oh, who can tell me?' And he set off on horseback to visit the good old man, who he thought might give him good counsel.

Night found him in the forest, and he lay down under the very trees where the faithful servant had first heard the winds talking. No, the prince cannot sleep; his troubled thoughts keep him wakeful. The winds are talking again, and the prince hears them.

'Good evening, brother, how fares it with you, brother?' says the wind from Spain.

'I do not feel easy, brother,' says the wind from France. 'Someone has twice overheard our secrets.'

'Then let us search and see that no one is listening tonight,' says the wind from Spain.

Then the two winds began to feel among the branches of the trees, and under the trees, with their long fingers. Those long fingers strayed over the hair on the prince's head; but they took the hair for moss. And they went back into the tree tops.

'There is no one here tonight,' says the wind from Spain. 'So what is the news, brother?'

And the wind from France answered, 'The prince has killed his faithful servant, who twice saved the princess Felicity from death. Now the prince repents: he would restore his servant to life if he could.'

'And is there no way of doing that?' said the wind from Spain.

'Yes, there is a way, but the prince will never know it. Near to the river bank where the faithful servant lies is the well of the water of life. The prince has but to sprinkle some of that water on his servant's forehead, and his servant will arise from the dead. But the prince does not know it, and so he will never do it.'

'No, he will never do it,' said the wind from Spain. 'Goodnight, brother!'

The two winds then drifted away, one to the south, the other to the north.

And in the forest was a great silence.

The prince leaped to his feet, sprang on his horse, and galloped back through the night. He galloped, galloped, and at dawn came to the river bank where the body of the faithful servant lay, with a riderless horse grazing beside it.

'Ah, my friend, my friend, how wickedly I have served you!'

cried the prince. 'But where is this well of the water of life that I may raise you from the dead?'

He looked round: he saw a little bird creeping in the dust of the road, dragging a broken wing. The little bird crept behind a slab of stone by the roadside. Now the prince could no longer see him; but in a moment there was the little bird again, perched on the stone, shaking bright water from his feathers, and singing with all his might.

'*Chiree, chiree, chiree!*' sang the little bird, opened both his wings, and flew away.

The prince hurried to the stone. Yes, there behind it was a well of sparkling water. He dipped his cupped hands into the well, brought them out filled with the sparkling water, ran, and sprinkled the water on to the forehead of the faithful servant.

The faithful servant opened his eyes; he gazed about him, he sprang to his feet. 'Ah, my master, how long I have slept!' said he.

And the prince humbled himself before the faithful servant, and knelt, and kissed his hand. 'Your *master?*' said he. 'Nay, from this day, your grateful brother!'

Then prince and servant rode back to the palace together. And the prince honoured the faithful servant, heaped riches upon him, and made him a lord.

11 · The White Cat and the Green Snake

A king and a queen had two daughters. One was called Roxana, the other Hespera. They were both beautiful; but Roxana was giddy and pert, and Hespera was quiet. And the king and queen thought more of the gay Roxana then they did of her quiet sister.

Now when the two princesses were just grown up, and it was time to find them husbands, the king and queen gave a magnificent ball. The ball was to last three nights, and all the princes and young lords of the neighbouring countries were invited.

At first these lords and princes asked to dance with Roxana; but they found her so pert and conceited, so aware of her charms – treating them as slaves to whom she condescended – that they danced with her only once, and then sought out Hespera. And Hespera was so gracious and so quietly pleasant that at the end of the first night's ball she had all the princes and young lords crowding about her, and Roxana was left almost alone.

That made the king very angry. *What*, his little pet Roxana to be slighted, and that slyboots Hespera thrusting herself forward! 'I won't have it!' said the king.

And he told Hespera that she wasn't behaving as a modest maiden should.

Poor Hespera! She was hurt. And at the next night's ball she tried to hide in a corner. But it was no good: the princes and the young lords sought her out. Dance with her they would, and dance with her they did.

And the king was still angry. 'I'll *make* these foolish gallants learn that Roxana comes first!' he said to the queen.

'But the gallants will do as they will do,' said the queen. 'You can't order them about.'

'Then I'll send Hespera away this very night!' cried the king. And he called her to him and said, 'My girl, you must leave this instant to visit your godmother.'

'But, Papa,' said Hespera, 'it is black night, I should be afraid all by myself in the dark, and I am very tired. Please let me wait till morning!'

'No,' said the king, 'you must go *at once*. I will give you a basket of food for the journey, and send a groom to go with you.'

Well, there was nothing more to be said. Hespera got on her white mare and rode off into the night, with a groom riding behind her.

They rode, rode, and they came to a forest; and Hespera was so tired, so tired, she could scarcely keep herself erect in the saddle. So she said to the groom, 'I would sleep a little, for I can go no farther.'

She got off her horse; the groom made her a bed of leaves and moss. Hespera lay down, the groom put the basket of food under her head for a pillow, and there she was next moment – fast asleep.

And what does the groom do? He jumps on his horse, takes Hespera's white mare by the rein, and gallops away. And in this he was only obeying the king's orders. For the king had told him he must do his best to lose poor Princess Hespera.

Hespera woke at sunrise. Where was she? All alone in the middle of a great forest. She jumped up and looked about her. No groom, no horses! She called, called, but no one answered. She took up her basket of provisions and walked on through the forest, hoping to reach her godmother's house. She walked all day. But the forest seemed endless, and when evening came again, she was completely lost.

'Perhaps if I climbed a tree,' she thought, 'I might see a light somewhere, a light from a woodman's hut where I might crave shelter.' So she climbed a tree, but saw no light. And feeling more desolate than ever, she spent the night in the tree.

Next morning she was awakened by a light shining in her eyes. What was it? Not the sun! It was something shining far off, and shining so brilliantly that it almost dazzled her. She came down from the tree and walked towards the light, and the nearer she got to it, the brighter it shone: a gleaming, blazing light, sparkling with many colours, and so blindingly bright that she had to put her hand before her face and peep at it through her fingers.

What could it be? A great fire? But no fire ever glowed with so many colours.

So, guided by that dazzling light, she came out of the forest, and there before her she saw a palace built all of coloured crystals that shone like jewels in the rising sun.

'Oh, oh, the beautiful palace!'

She went up some crystal steps and knocked at a crystal door. But no one came to answer it. She knocked a second time: still no answer. She knocked a third time, and heard a patter of little foot-steps, and little voices that spoke like music.

She peeped through the crystal door and saw, scampering down a crystal staircase, a throng of tiny men. These tiny men were only a cubit high. And so Little Cubits we will call them.

Six Little Cubits, standing on each other's shoulders, lifted the latch of the door. Six more Little Cubits pulled the door open. 'Who are you?' they said to Hespera.

'I am Hespera, a king's daughter. I have been lost in the forest. I ask your kind permission to come in and rest.'

'Enter,' said the Little Cubits. 'We will lead you to our mistress, and ask her permission for you to rest here.'

They led her through many crystal halls and corridors, and brought her at last to a throne room, where their mistress, a beautiful white cat, lay curled up on a golden chair. 'What is it you ask of me?' said the White Cat to Hespera.

'Just to rest my aching limbs for a little while, my lady,' said Hespera.

'And what will you do when your aching limbs are rested?'

'I don't know,' said poor Hespera; and the tears trickled down her cheeks.

'You may stay with me if you wish,' said the White Cat. 'But only if you will give me your promise not to go away without my permission, and to obey me in all things.'

'I will gladly promise that, my lady,' said Hespera.

'Come, bring a meal here for the princess,' said the White Cat to the Little Cubits.

The Little Cubits hurried to obey. Four of them came carrying a tray of food on their shoulders; three of them came carrying a bottle of wine; two others carried a glass. Three Little Cubits stood on each other's shoulders to spread the cloth and lay the table. And the princess Hespera sat down and ate.

'Did you find the food to your liking?' said the White Cat when Hespera had finished.

'Ah, yes indeed, my lady!'

'Then come, I will show you my garden.'

And the White Cat led Hespera out into a garden, so big, so big there seemed no end to it, with grass so green and smooth, with trees so gracious, with flowers so beautiful that Hespera clapped her hands in delight.

'You see that my garden is large,' said the White Cat. 'You may wander about in it at your will. You may pick the fruit and the flowers. But I forbid you to go near the lake that shines yonder beyond the trees. If you disobey me, I shall know of it. And you will not be long in repenting it.'

'I will not disobey you, my lady,' said Hespera.

And she meant what she said.

So Hespera lived with the White Cat for some time, wandering about the lovely garden, picking the fruit and the flowers. In a way she was happy: but often she felt lonely. For the White Cat had a haughty manner with her; and was, moreover, often absent for days at a time. And the Little Cubits, though they attended to all Hespera's wants, and were friendly in their fashion, yet regarded her as someone to serve, and not as a companion.

And Hespera longed for a companion.

As she wandered about the garden she would often look towards the waters of the lake that gleamed beyond a fringe of trees. 'I wonder why I am forbidden to go there?' she thought. And the more often she thought this, the more curious she became. She would stand for a long time looking through that belt of trees to the distant water, whose brightness seemed to be beckoning her.

Now one very hot noonday, when the flowers drooped their heads and even the birds were silent, Hespera sought shelter among the belt of trees from the heat of the sun; and without thinking, wandered on in the direction of the lake, and so came at last out from under the trees on to a lawn that sloped down towards the water.

'Oh dear, I mustn't go a step farther!' she told herself.

Then a little breeze blew from the lake, a cool little breeze that fanned her hot cheeks and seemed to be whispering, 'Come, come – why not?'

'And after all, why not?' thought Hespera. 'Now I have come so far it were surely foolish to turn back. No one will ever know: the Little Cubits are busy about the palace, and the White Cat has gone away, and won't be home till evening.'

And she went down to the lake.

Shimmering water ruffled by the breeze, golden reeds gently swaying in the breeze, and, near the bank, a cluster of white water-lilies gleaming in the sun. It was all very pretty, but there was nothing special about that lake. Hespera sighed. What had she expected? She scarcely knew.

'I wish I hadn't come,' she said to herself. 'Now I have broken my word – and all for nothing! I will go back quickly, and never come here again.'

But even as she turned to go, a big green snake slid from under the water-lilies and darted to her feet.

'Princess, princess,' said the Green Snake, 'do not run from me! Indeed, indeed I will do you no harm! If you are lonely, I am lonelier! Will you not stay and talk to me? It is so long, so long since I have spoken to a living soul.'

And he looked up at her so wistfully out of his jewel-like eyes, that Hespera stooped and stroked his head.

'Poor snake!' she said. 'Yes, I will stay, but only for a little while.'

And she sat down by the edge of the lake, and the Green Snake laid his head in her lap.

So they talked together. Hespera told the Green Snake what it was like to live lonely in a palace with only a haughty White Cat and some Little Cubits for company. And the Green Snake told

Hespera what it was like to live lonely under the water-lilies with
no company at all. And one word leading to another word, there
they were talking together till the sun went down beyond the lake
and dew dampened the grass, and Hespera leaped to her feet and
cried, 'Oh, I must go! I must go!'

'But you will come again?' said the Green Snake. 'Promise me
that you will come again!'

'I don't know. Indeed, indeed, I can promise nothing,' answered
Hespera, and fled swift as any hare back to the palace.

And there at the palace door, stands the White Cat.

'Hespera, where have you been?'

'Just – just walking in the garden, my lady.'

'Yes,' says the White Cat, 'you have been walking in the garden;
but in spite of my having forbidden it, you have also been to the
lake. Little Cubits! Little Cubits! Take this bad girl and plunge
her into boiling milk.'

The Little Cubits came running; they undressed poor Hespera
and plunged her into a bath of steaming milk. But they shed tears
as they did it, and perhaps their tears cooled the milk a little. At
any rate, though the pain was very terrible, Hespera was not so
fearfully burned as you might imagine. And when the Little Cubits
had taken her out of the bath, they soothed her blistered skin with
healing ointment, and laid her in her bed, and took such care of
her that it wasn't long before she was completely cured.

Nor was it long, despite all she had suffered, before she went
down to the lake again. For all the time that she had lain in bed it
seemed to her that she heard the Green Snake calling her, and that
the Green Snake was saying, 'Hespera! Hespera! If you don't come
to me again, I shall surely die!'

'And I *will* come to you again!' thought Hespera. 'Who is the
White Cat that she should forbid me?'

And so, one day when the White Cat was away, Hespera ran to
the lake.

The Green Snake was lying on the grass at the water's edge.

He had grown very thin. 'I thought you had forgotten me,' he said in a feeble voice. 'And I have been ill, dear Hespera.'

'Ah,' said Hespera, 'and I have been badly punished, dear snake.'

And she sat down, took his head in her lap, and talked to him, forgetting how the time passed, till twilight fell. And then she jumped up in a fright and ran back to the palace.

There is the White Cat standing at the door.

'Again! Again!' growls the White Cat. 'You have disobeyed me again! Little Cubits, take this wicked girl and plunge her into a bath of boiling oil.'

The Little Cubits come running. They undress poor Hespera and plunge her into a bath of boiling oil. Their tears fall like rain over her scalded body, and there is healing pity in their tears. They carry her to her bed, soothe her blistered skin with healing ointment, and care for her most tenderly.

However she was ill for a long time.

And one day, when she had just been able to rise from her bed and sit in a chair by the window, she heard a rustling, and there was the Green Snake crawling slowly towards her. He looked so terribly ill, so terribly ill that she cried out, 'Oh, my Green Snake! Oh, my poor Green Snake!'

'Yes, I am sick nigh unto death,' said the Green Snake. 'But it is in your power to cure me, Hespera.'

'Oh, how? Tell me but how?'

'Take me for your husband.'

'Dear snake, what you ask me is impossible!'

'Do you not love me?' said the Green Snake.

'Yes, in a way I love you,' said Hespera. 'But to take you for my husband, dear snake – ah, that is a very different matter!'

So the Green Snake crawled sadly away. The next day he came again, asked the same question, got the same answer, and crawled sadly away. He came again and again, and every time he came he was thinner and weaker. And though Hespera wept to see him,

she still said that to take him for her husband was impossible
And by and by the Green Snake came no more.

'Oh, what can have happened to him?' thought Hespera. And
(since she was by this time well again) heedless of anything the
White Cat might do to her, she ran to the lake.

The Green Snake lay on the grass, his body shrunk and stick-
like, his eyes closed. He neither moved nor spoke.

'My snake! My snake!' cried Hespera.

The Green Snake opens his eyes. Ah, how pitifully he looks at
her. 'I am dying, Hespera,' he whispers.

'No, no, *no*!' cries Hespera. 'You shall *not* die! If it will cure you,
my darling snake, here and now I promise to take you for my
husband!'

Oh! Oh! What was happening? Earth and sky, lawn and lake –
the whole world was spinning round her. She could neither see nor
hear nor think. And then suddenly she seemed to awake from a
dream. Where was she, and who was it that held her in his arms?
There were people laughing, there were people cheering, there
were people shouting for joy.

'Hespera, Hespera, my bride! Hespera, Hespera, our princess!
Hespera, Hespera, my daughter!'

Yes, Hespera seemed to wake from a dream to find herself
surrounded by a company of merry lords and ladies, to see a
stately queen, wearing a diamond crown and a white fur robe,
who smiled and called her 'daughter', and – best of all – to be
clasped in the arms of a handsome prince, a handsome prince
dressed all in glittering green.

But – the White Cat, the Little Cubits, the Green Snake, where
had they gone?

'I am the White Cat,' said the stately queen.

'We are the Little Cubits,' cried the merry lords and ladies.

'Hespera, dear Hespera, I am the Green Snake,' said the glittering
prince. 'A wicked wizard bound us all with his evil spells: spells
only to be broken on the day that a princess consented to marry a

Green Snake. He thought that day would never come. But you, my Hespera, have broken the spell. Ah, blessed be the time when our father drove you away from home and brought you to our palace!'

'But I have done nothing,' said Hespera. 'Except to be a little disobedient!'

'And thereby to be our deliverer,' said the queen. 'Hespera, forgive me that I was severe with you, forgive me that I punished you so cruelly! I could do no other, for such were the magician's orders.'

'I have already forgotten it,' said Hespera.

What more to be told? Hespera married her glittering green-clad prince; they held a wedding feast in the palace of many-coloured crystals.

And all the world rejoiced.

12 · Rags and Tatters

There was an old king who had one son and three daughters
And when the time came for this old king to die, he called the
prince, his son, to him and said, 'Dear son, in a few hours the
kingdom will be yours. Govern it well and wisely. You have
already a good wife to help you, but your three sisters are still
unmarried. As soon as I am dead, go out on to the terrace and
pick a rose from the rose bush that grows there. Throw the rose
down into the street. And the man who picks it up shall have
your eldest sister to wife. Pick another rose and throw it from the
terrace; the man who picks it up shall be the husband of your
second sister. Pick yet a third rose, and throw it down; and who
ever picks it up shall be the husband of your youngest sister. Give
me your promise that you will do exactly as I bid you; and so I
may die happy.'

'Father, I will obey you in all things.'

And the old king died happy.

Then the prince, who was now king, went out on to the terrace,
plucked a rose from the bush that grew there, threw it down into
the street, and set a soldier to guard it. And very soon a duke
came driving by in his carriage, saw the rose, jumped out of his
carriage, picked up the rose and put it in his buttonhole.

And the soldier on guard said to the duke, 'Our lord the king
would speak with your grace.'

So the duke went up on to the terrace; the young king sent for
his eldest sister; she pleased the duke, the duke pleased her; they
were married that very day, and the duke drove off with his bride.

118

Next morning the young king plucked another rose and threw
t down into the street. Very soon a handsome lord came riding
by. He jumped off his horse, picked up the rose, and put it in his
buttonhole. And the soldier on guard said to him, 'My lord, the
king would speak with you.'

So the handsome lord went up on to the terrace. The young king
ent for his second sister; she pleased the handsome lord, the handsome lord pleased her. They were married that very day, and the
handsome lord rode off with his bride.

Next morning the young king plucked yet a third rose, and threw
t down into the street. And who should come walking by but a
water-carrier called Rags and Tatters. The water-carrier's shoulders
were bowed under a thick pole, with a heavy barrel hanging from
either end of it; his coat was full of holes, and his legs were bound
up with rags. When he saw the rose, he hitched the pole from his
shoulders, set down his barrels, stooped and picked up the rose.

'Why, Rags and Tatters, Rags and Tatters,' laughed the soldier
on guard, 'you must come up on to the terrace, for I think my lord
the king would speak with you.'

So Rags and Tatters went up on to the terrace, and the young
king sent for his youngest sister. 'This is the man you must marry,'
said he.

Well, well, here was a fine sort of husband for a proud little
princess! She said, 'I won't marry him, I *won't*!'

But the young king, her brother, said, 'I cannot break the
promise I gave to my father.' So the youngest princess was married
to Rags and Tatters, and she cried all through the wedding.

Rags and Tatters walked off with his bride. They walked,
walked, walked, till the princess's feet were sore, and they came to
a wretched little straw hut.

'Dear wife,' said Rags and Tatters, 'this is our home.'

Now in those days a wife must do as her husband told her. And
what this princess had to do was to cook and clean and scrub and
wash the linen. So she soon got her fine clothes into a pretty mess.

Rags and Tatters told her to take them off, and he gave her a coarse woollen dress and a sackcloth apron to work in. And she wept and wept.

Every morning Rags and Tatters rose at dawn, and went off with his pole and his water barrels, leaving the princess alone in the straw hut. And she wept as she cleaned the kitchen, she wept as she washed the clothes, she wept as she prepared the supper. And when Rags and Tatters came home in the evening, she wept as she unwrapt the rags from about his legs and washed his feet. Her lovely eyes were always red, her cheeks always swollen and wet with tears. She looked a real fright. And Rags and Tatters, who loved her more than his life, was sorely grieved.

'Dear wife,' said he, 'won't you try to be happy?'

'No, I will *not* try,' said she – and went to bed weeping.

In the night she dreamed: she dreamed that she was in a wonderful palace, where many finely-dressed servants waited on her. And she dreamed that she stepped into a golden coach, drawn by six splendid horses, and set off to visit the young king, her brother. But when she woke in the morning, there she was back in the straw hut, lying on a lumpy mattress.

And she told Rags and Tatters what she had dreamed.

Rags and Tatters laughed and said, 'What should a water-carrier's wife be doing in a palace? Put the dream out of your head!' So the princess wept all day. She went to bed still weeping.

And when she woke in the morning – where was she? She was lying in a silken bed in a magnificent room in the wonderful palace she had dreamed of the night before. Soft-stepping maidens made ready her bath of scented water, and dressed her in royal robes. And when she was dressed she went down into the prettiest of pretty little parlours, where lacqueys in silk and velvet brought her her breakfast. And when she had eaten, the head lacquey said, 'What orders has her Royal Highness for today?'

And she answered, 'Order my coach to be brought round. I wish to pay a visit to the king, my brother.'

The head lacquey bowed low and went out. Very soon he came back, and said, 'The coach awaits your Royal Highness.'

So the princess stepped daintily down the marble staircase, and came to the door of the palace. There in the courtyard stood a golden coach, drawn by six magnificent snow-white horses. And the princess stepped into the coach, and drove off to visit her brother.

The young king was standing on the terrace. He looked down and saw the golden coach draw up at his gates. 'Dear me,' said he to himself, 'who can be coming to visit me in such style?' And then – who should step out of the coach but his youngest sister!

So he ran full of joy and amazement to meet her. 'Dear sister,' said he, 'is it really you? How have you brought about all this magnificence? And where is your husband?'

'I don't know where he is,' pouted the princess. 'But I am living in a palace; and I have come to invite you and your queen, and my sisters and their husbands to dine with me today.'

So messengers were sent to summon the princess's two sisters and their two husbands – the duke and the handsome lord. And then the king and his queen, the princess's sisters, the duke and the lord all set out with a great retinue to the youngest sister's palace, where they found a finely spread table and sat down to a splendid feast. But when the feast was nearly over, the duke happened to look up at the ceiling.

What did he see? He saw a hole open in the ceiling, and through that hole Rags and Tatters was smiling down on them. 'Look – look up there!' cried the duke. 'Surely that is Rags and Tatters?'

But the guests had hardly time to cry 'Oh!' when Rags and Tatters vanished, the whole palace fell in with a crash, the king and his queen, the sisters and their husbands found themselves at home again. And as for the youngest sister – there she was in the straw hut, in her woollen gown and her sackcloth apron.

Oh how she wept! Rags and Tatters came home in the evening and found her still weeping. She told him all her grief, and he laughed and said, 'Ah, can't you be content with dreaming by night, but must go dreaming also in broad daylight? Come now, my dearest wife, unwrap my legs and wash my feet, and say that you love me just a little. For I love you so much that I would gladly die for you.'

But she only said, 'Oh, how unhappy I am!'

And Rags and Tatters sighed.

So a few days passed; and one night, the princess, tired out with her heavy day's work, again went to bed weeping. She fell asleep weeping. But when she woke in the morning – where was she? Back in the wonderful palace, lying in the silken bed, surrounded by her soft-stepping ladies-in-waiting. And all happened as it had happened before: she bathed, dressed, breakfasted, ordered out her golden coach, drove off to visit the king, her brother, summoned her sisters and their husbands, and brought them all back to feast in her palace.

And when the feast was nearly over, the young king happened to look up at the ceiling. What did he see? He saw a hole open in the ceiling: and there was Rags and Tatters looking down through the hole, and laughing. 'Look, look, sister, look up there! Surely that is your husband, Rags and Tatters!'

But Rags and Tatters vanished, the palace fell in, the king and his queen, the sisters and their husbands found themselves at home again. . . . And the youngest sister, dressed in her old woollen gown, was sitting in the straw hut, weeping.

That evening, when Rags and Tatters came home, she told him all that had happened, and said, 'Surely, my husband, you must be to blame?'

'No, I am not to blame,' said Rags and Tatters. 'You dream by day as well as by night. Can I help it?'

'I don't know,' said the princess, 'I don't know!' And there she was weeping again. But Rags and Tatters took her in his arms, and told her how dearly he loved her. And she stopped weeping.

So a month passed; and every day it seemed to the princess that Rags and Tatters was growing handsomer; and every day it seemed to her that she was getting fonder of him. 'If it were not for his rags, he might be a prince,' she thought. 'And though I am the wife of a poor drudge, he is not to blame for that. He is always kind. I will try not to weep any more. I will try to smile and please him.' And she did smile, and she did please him.

So one evening, after she had unwound the rags from his legs and washed his feet, she raised up her lovely face and kissed him. And Rags and Tatters cried out, 'Oh my princess, my beautiful princess, you do at last love me a little?'

And the princess said, 'I love you more than a little, my husband.'

That night, when she went to bed, the princess did not weep: she lay and slept like a good child, calm and smiling.

In the morning she woke – where was she? Back in her splendid palace. 'Today I know what I must do,' she thought. 'I will invite my brother and his wife, and my sisters and their husbands to a feast as I have done before. But they shall only come on one condition: that if my husband should choose to look down upon us as we sit feasting, no one shall cry out, "Look, there is Rags and Tatters!" No one shall be so discourteous as to call him by that ugly name. What he does is his own affair; and he shall do it without comment from anybody.'

So she drove out in her golden coach and invited her guests to a feast, as she had done before. But she warned them that no one must look up at the ceiling, or cry out, 'Look, look, there is Rags and Tatters!' And they all promised that they would not.

Well, they sat and feasted as usual; and when the feast was nearly over, the ceiling opened and Rags and Tatters looked down. And he was laughing. But even when they heard the laughter, no one looked up: they just went on eating and drinking and talking loudly, as if nothing had happened.

So Rags and Tatters went away; the hole in the ceiling closed; and next moment who should appear among the astonished guests but a princely young man dressed in royal robes and wearing a gold coronet. None of the guests knew him; but the princess knew him. And she ran to him and cried, 'My husband, my husband, by what name shall I call you?'

'I am Alfonso, prince of Spain,' said he, 'condemned by an evil witch to take the shape of a ragged water-carrier, until in that shape, a royal princess should wed me, and in that shape come to love me. You have freed me, my beloved wife; and now whenever you wish I can take you home.'

Then they all rejoiced, and held a three-day festival in the splendid palace. And at the end of the festival prince Alfonso, son of the king of Spain, set out with his lovely wife to travel home. They travelled in the golden coach drawn by the six prancing white horses; but as soon as they had left the splendid palace, that palace disappeared. Where it had been sprang up a garden; and in the garden roses bloomed of such loveliness as the world had never seen before, nor ever will see again.

13 · Stupid Head

A prince was walking in a wood, and feeling hot and tired he sat down under a tree to rest. And as he so sat, he heard people talking up in the tree.

'Who can be talking up there?' thought the prince. And he began to climb the tree to find out where the voices were coming from. He climbed, climbed, and – what do you think? – he came to a village. The villagers were busy building up some houses that the wind had blown down, and they called on the prince to help them. But the prince said, 'No, having come up so far, I've a mind to go higher.'

And he climbed and he climbed till he came to the very top of the tree; and then what should he see but a fine palace.

The palace doors were open, the prince went in. He went from room to room, and there were hobgoblins in every room, and they were all asleep. But in the uppermost room of all there was a princess bound to a pillar by a gold chain.

'Oh, oh!' cried the princess. 'Set me free and I'll love you for ever more!'

'But who has chained you up?' asked the prince.

'Old Stupid Head, a hideous hobgoblin with bat's wings,' said the princess. 'But he's away now at his sister's wedding. Quick, quick, set me free, and let us be off before he comes back!'

The prince looked about him and found a hatchet. He hacked through a link of the gold chain and freed the princess. He took her by the hand and they ran out of the palace, scrambled down the tree and were racing away through the wood, when Stupid Head came flying back to his palace.

When he found all the hobgoblins asleep and the princess gone didn't Stupid Head scream with rage! He ran through the palace slapping and pinching the hobgoblins till they too were screaming and then he rushed out and bounced down the tree from branch to branch till he came to the village.

'Has the princess passed this way?' he shrieked.

'Yes,' said the people, 'she passed this way only ten minutes ago.'

They were going to tell him that a prince was with her, but he wouldn't stop to listen. He was down out of that tree and rushing through the wood in the wink of an eye. He was roaring and screaming, and the prince and princess heard him. The princess jumped into a bush and hid; the prince, who still had the hatchet in his hand, bent down and began chopping up some wood.

Stupid Head took him for a woodcutter and shouted, 'Have you seen a princess running this way?'

It seemed the prince didn't hear him. The prince was pretending to be deaf. And he was pretending to sob and moan, too. 'Oh! Oh! O-oh!'

'*Have you seen a princess pass this way?*' screamed Stupid Head.

'Oh! Oh! Oh!' sobbed the prince.

'HAVE YOU SEEN A PRINCESS?' yelled Stupid Head louder and louder.

'How should I see any one?' blubbered the prince. 'My eyes are blind with tears. I have been weeping all the morning. Ah me! Ah me! Haven't you heard the terrible news? The valiant Stupid Head is sick and like to die!'

'Oh lor!' cried Stupid Head. 'That's terrible news indeed! But can it be true?'

And he rushed away back with him to his palace at the top of the tree. He pounced on the hobgoblins and shook them till their teeth rattled.

'Am I sick and like to die?' he screamed.

'No, you are not sick!' cried the hobgoblins. 'You are as well and strong as can be.'

'Then I'll kill that lying woodcutter, I will, I will!' shouted Stupid Head, and off with him down the tree again.

The prince and princess were running, running. They heard Stupid Head crashing through the wood after them. The princess crept into a fox's hole; the prince turned his coat inside out, put his cap on back to front, and hurried to meet Stupid Head.

'Have you seen a woodcutter and a princess pass this way?' shouted Stupid Head.

'I have seen no one,' said the prince. 'And I have no time to stand gossiping. I am the king's messenger, and I am hurrying to carry the sad news to the hobgoblins in Stupid Head's palace.'

'What sad news?' shouted Stupid Head.

'Oh, haven't you heard? The valiant Stupid Head is dead.'

When Stupid Head heard that, he rushed away back to his palace at the top of the tree. He snatched up the hobgoblins one after the other, shook them, slapped them, boxed their ears.

'Am I dead? Am I dead?' he screamed.

'You were never more alive,' sobbed the hobgoblins.

'Oh! Oh! Oh! What lies people tell!' shrieked Stupid Head. And down the tree with him again, and chasing through the wood after the prince and princess.

But the prince and princess were running fast. They got clear of the wood and reached the prince's palace, just as Stupid Head caught up with them. Stupid Head made a grab at the princess's robe, but she slipped out of it and ran up the palace steps in her petticoat. The prince flung the hatchet at Stupid Head, pulled the princess through the palace door, and slammed and bolted it.

Stupid Head crept back to his tree. He had a great bump on his forehead where the hatchet had hit him. Yes, he was sick and sorry now, if he hadn't been sick and sorry before.

The prince and princess laughed and laughed. And then they kissed each other and decided to get married.

So they held a merry wedding and lived happily ever after.